IELTS

一次就考到

雅思文法

突破寫作盲點且即刻茅塞頓開

韋爾◎著

三大學習特色 釐清寫作未達7分主因／詳盡解析並搭配超值背誦音檔／長難句雙效強化寫作和閱讀

辨別文法正誤：藉由文法**「正誤句」**提升察覺寫作**「盲點」**的能力，克服卡住雅思寫作6.5分的瓶頸，一舉獲取高分。

詳盡文法解析：釐清各種**文句搭配**，迅速找出長句中的主、動詞，在閱讀時，靈活運用**「跳讀」**等技巧，**迅速拆解試題**。

長難句強化：書中文法關鍵句的衍伸均為長難句設計，藉由文法同步提升閱讀時**「長難句理解」**和寫作中**「多樣句型」**的表達。

EDITOR 作者序

對於大多數的亞洲考生來說，雅思寫作的備考是頗具挑戰的。當然，當中有少數在國外待過數年或程度極好的考生一次就考取雅思寫作 7 分以上的成績，但對於大多數備考的考生來說，許多人卡在雅思寫作 6.5 分的瓶頸而百思不得其解。甚至也有不少外文系的考生也卡在了雅思寫作 6.5 分的魔咒中。儘管演練了更多劍橋官方雅思寫作題目也請老師更改了，但再次應考時卻仍是獲取雅思寫作 6.5 分的成績。幾經努力後，轉而將重心轉到衝高雅思「閱讀」和「聽力」上。這樣來回數次後，已經花了許多錢在報名費上。而在這些備考中，許多甚至產生了「自我懷疑」或者是質疑著在修了 4-6 堂外文系寫作課後，仍無法考取雅思寫作 7 分的成績，所以那到底該相信什麼呢？（而坊間也有太多書籍的範文，如果你拿去詢問考取雅思寫作高分的考生或外籍生時，卻會換來白眼，因為照這樣的方式寫並不會使你得到預期的理想成績）。在備考當中，也有許多考生開始神化了那些考取高分的考生，而產生了「妄自菲薄」的心理，反而影響了備考。如果時間回到求學時期，我可能也會有這樣類似的想法。但隨著步入職場、閱讀一些書籍像是《刻意練習》等，以及更認識那些考取雅思平均 8 分的考生後，我越來越意識到，實際上根本不是這樣的。

以都就讀頂大外文系的 A、B、C 三位考生為例好了，三位都沒有當過交換生、待過國外數年的經驗和補習雅思（所以這三位都是在同個雅思備考起點的），而且從小到大在英文科的表現都很優異，在大學課堂中也都認真學習，均接受同樣的課程訓練，儘管在校內英文寫作分數上有著些微差異，但三個人程度相似，並不會因為誰這寫作分數上多誰兩分，就真的能看出誰較為優秀。於大肆那年，三位均報考了雅思考試，在寫作單項上的成績分別是 7.5, 7.0, 6.5 分，是蠻大的差異。而稍後，C 在準備一段時間後又考取了雅思 6.5 分，他感到不可思議，也不禁懷疑著難道 A 和 B 均比自己優秀嗎？（而在雅思寫作跟口說單項上，有時候確實要多個 0.5 分又是要花了數個月的努力跟改進才能達到的。雅思考試確實在評分上有一定的準度，而且壁壘分明，也不會像新多益那樣靠題海策略等，準備後，突然應考就考到某個分數段）。

既然是這樣的話，那...，而眾多的考少均屬於 C 類型，（有的幾經掙扎或又準備了半年後，找到了突破點，獲取雅思七分。有的，念了語言學校一陣子後，考到了雅思寫作 7 分的成績。...）。案例中的 C，從起初的疑惑，轉向詢問 A 如何考到該成績的，而當然 A 也據實以答，僅說就是照著學校的課程，也沒特別準備什麼就考到了雅思寫作 7.5 的成績，但是對於 C 和眾多 C 類型的學習者，這樣的答案是很難令人信服的。

（不過我能懂 A 的那種感覺，有時候真的無法解釋為什麼有辦法考到，且並不是不願意協助別人、想看別人卡在某個分數段更久或要對方請吃大餐才願意分享經驗。）C 像是摸摸鼻子走了般，改由衝高「閱讀」和「聽力」的分數，讓全部平均都拉高，考到分數就要開始申請學校了。（對於像 C 這樣的學習者，我覺得是很可惜的）隨著更了解這項考試等等的以及雅思壁壘分明的評分，雖然在成績單上，分數上確實是不同，不過我後來覺得是一樣的。因為還有太多因素影響考試結果。而覺得自己掌握要訣的考生，其實也沒有真的掌握要訣，例如：**我懂，如果要考更高分，我必須在圖表題中比較數個重點，凸顯其中重點的相似處或相異處。**（確實是如此沒錯，但考生即使比較了，或使用比較級等，仍是卡在某個分數段，主因是沒有掌握關鍵點，所以這也是這本**「雅思文法」**規劃的主因）。

回到認為「A 跟 C 兩者能力其實相同的論述」，我想讀者或考生會很驚訝，會認為明明就不同，也沒辦法比。所以我覺得必須要探討還可能影響的因素（就像是在面試後，儘管能力相似，有的工作就需要更 detail-oriented 的工作者，有的甚至會在人力銀行工作介紹中就會表明。）而像 A 這樣的學習者，其實能考到更高分的原因，並不是更優秀，只是更注意細節（或更擅長寫作等等，確實每個人在學習語言上，有的人會在閱讀類更為擅長，有的會更需要聽力輔助學習等等的，這些背後影響的原因，也會影響這些單項備考時間），而也認為別人也會注意到這些細節。在英文寫作中，確實有太多細節點要注意，而這些細節點就是眾多 C 類型學習者忽略的，但是只要有人去**統整這些細節點**，C 也能迅速考到跟 A 一樣的成績（因為 C 類型的學習者在英文的語句表達中已經有了一定的根基）。有些 C 類型的考生，是經由又補習了一年，從每次外籍老師的批改作文（可能每周一篇或兩周一篇），累積這些被批改用語「錯誤」的地方（**細節點**），到了一定的作文數量時，其實就剛好能突破了某個寫作關卡。但其實有人**整合**這些細節點，就能大幅**「縮短」**備考時間了，考生不需要花費這些時間和經由作文批改的累積（有的是在學校課堂 4-6 學期的寫作課中，不斷地完善自己的表達），直接看整理好的注意點，避免會造成失分的部分即可。

而對於像 C 類型的學習者，我的想法是，比起更高分的學習者，其實自己本身並沒有不如那些學習者，而如果從小到到英文都不錯，藉由這些細節點等的改進（你只是在重複考數次的中間，沒有人告訴你這些重點），你也能在更短的時間內，獲取像 A 類型的學習者同樣的成績。

（你也值得申請上更好的學校）

回到考生知道要比較「相似處」或「相異處」但仍卡在某分數段的問題。我想，考生不能悲觀的想成，我有使用比較級了，但是考官還是給我 6.5 分，所以我認了，或者是高分考生跟我這樣講，但還是沒有用呀！。所以我們從一個文法例子來看好了，例如：Before the rainy season, carnivores have a much better life than herbivores.在例句中，這樣的比較是無誤的，**carnivores** 是肉食性動物，而 **herbivores** 是草食性動物，兩者的關係是對等的。但是在另一個例子時（也是考生覺得在圖表題中使用了數句的比較級，但分數並無提升的情況，這幾次的應考中，考生只是持續地使用錯誤的句子），Before the rainy season, the life of the carnivores is much worse than herbivores.（在這個例句中，考生未注意到細節點，即**「比較對象」**不同了，又因為本身非母語人士，很自然地認為這個句子沒有文法問題，時態也正確，但是其實卻犯了修飾上的錯誤）。因為**「肉食動物的生活/**the life of the carnivores」和**「草食性動物/**herbivores」是無法比較的，應該要改成**「草食性動物的生活」**才能做比較。錯誤句中僅使用了 herbivores，要修正為 the life of herbivores/**that of herbivores**.才對。（that 和 those 的用法和指代，其實在國中文法中就教過，所以是指代前方出現過的 **the life**）。最後希望考生也能夠多演練寫作試題、與高分學習者請益等等，並運用書中提到的 150 則文法提點和各式句型表達，在最短時間內獲取雅思寫作高分。

韋爾 敬上

INSTRUCTIONS

使用說明

Unit 59
Unlike ❷：加形容詞子句修飾

正誤句

KEY 59

✖ Unlike desert lizards, which bury themselves under the sand, some forests can run onto the water for several miles to evade predators, such as snakes. Some lizards even have evolved to mimic gestures from other animals to ensure the survival.

◯ Unlike desert lizards, which bury themselves under the sand, some forest lizards can run onto the water for several miles to evade predators, such as snakes. Some lizards even have evolved to mimic gestures from other animals to ensure the survival.

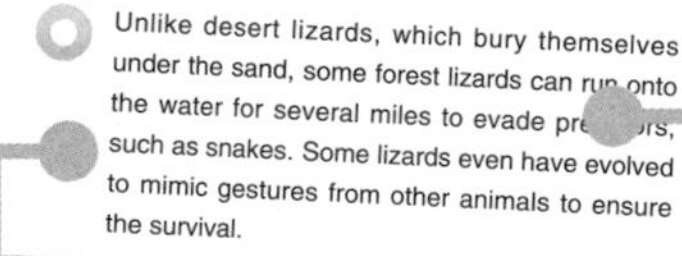

中　譯：不像沙漠的蜥蜴，將其埋在沙子底下，有些森林的蜥蜴能夠在水面上跑幾哩以逃避掠食者，像是蛇。有些蜥蜴甚至已經演化出模仿其他動物的姿勢來確保其生存。

解　析：除了前個單元的比較對象的用法，這個單元的句型是前個句型的進階用法，在使用 **unlike+N** 後，再以一個**形容詞子句**來修飾該名詞，豐富表達。在句型中可以看見一個形容詞子句修飾 desert lizards，子句中的語意也是正確的。主要子句中的名詞就是跟 unlike 後的名詞做比較，錯誤句中使用了 some forests 造成語法上和語意上的錯誤，而且 forests **無法執行後面動詞所表達的動作**。

檢測考點：unlike 的用法、形容詞子句、表列舉。

佳句複誦

MP3 059

Unlike desert lizards, **which** bury themselves under the sand, some forest lizards can run onto the water for several miles to evade predators, such as snakes. Some lizards even have evolved to mimic gestures from other animals to ensure the survival.

STEP 1：【找出卡分的癥結點】

- 從**「錯誤句」**中糾錯，先檢視自己判斷句子的能力，是否能察覺出句子中的**「細節性錯誤」**，因為細節性錯誤往往是分數卡關的主因，例如：❶代名詞指涉的錯誤，可能會因為某個文法觀念的錯誤，造成在兩篇作文中，各式句型中有代名詞指涉的部分出現錯誤，累積起來的錯誤量（如果以**紅筆**都圈起來）其實是很可觀的。

STEP 2：【對照解析、釐清文法觀念】

- 如果能找出錯誤的地方，恭喜你，這是值得嘉許的！不過如果未能找出錯誤的地方，請也別氣餒，看**「正確句」**和**「解析」**檢視問題點，別讓這些**「問題點」**」影響你獲取高分。（很多時候其實就是在**比較句型**不斷地出現重複的錯誤，可能一篇文章中出現了數次比較上的錯誤，修正後分數就提高了）

STEP 3：【初步強化文法審查力、修正語句表達】

- 除了作者出題的**「錯誤句」**之外，你還需要不斷演練，在其他句子中也檢視類似的**「出題考點」**，訓練自己的文法力，強化這部分，例如：❶每個句子都演練找出**「主要主詞」**和**「主要動詞」**，找出句中的主要主詞和動詞是學習英文中很重要的一個部分，這影響到閱讀和寫作等等，而且要找得非常迅速。

STEP 4：【累積綜合文法能力、進階運用在「跳讀」上】

- 除了上述的演練之外，也務必要演練其他**「文法考點」**的檢查。經由這些綜合文法的快速檢視後，已經替你累積了更多的文法和閱讀實力。例如：在**「找主要主詞和動詞」**和**「同位語」**的部分好了，無形中會加快了你的閱讀速度，你可以進一步地演練**「跳讀」**的部分，看主詞後直接眼睛跳到閱讀動詞的部分，在寫劍橋雅思閱讀試題時，進一步實證有跳讀後所省略的閱讀時間。

STEP 5：【音檔神強化、內建「寫作腦」】

- 於零碎的時間，利用書籍中的音檔，持續性的強化語句表達，並於寫雅思作文試題時，不斷修正語句表達跟提升語句豐富度，書中收錄非常多樣的句式，在兩類型的作文中各能用到至少 **5-6** 個不同句式，等同於達到了雅思寫作 **7** 分的要求。

STEP 6：【翻譯和英文寫作能力飆升】

- 如果備考的時間還很充分的話，可以利用書中的正確句和中譯演練**「中譯英」**和**「英譯中」**，看著中譯檢視能否於空白筆記本上寫出正確的英文句子等等，同步強化**「翻譯」**和**「英文寫作」**實力。

Unit 59
Unlike ❷：加形容詞子句修飾

KEY 59

✖ Unlike desert lizards, which bury themselves under the sand, some forests can run onto the water for several miles to evade predators, such as snakes. Some lizards even have evolved to mimic gestures from other animals to ensure the survival.

○ Unlike desert lizards, which bury themselves under the sand, some forest lizards can run onto the water for several miles to evade predators, such as snakes. Some lizards even have evolved to mimic gestures from other animals to ensure the survival.

中　譯 不像沙漠的蜥蜴，將其埋在沙子底下，有些森林的蜥蜴能夠在水面上跑幾哩以逃避掠食者，像是蛇。有些蜥蜴甚至已經演化出模仿其他動物的姿勢來確保其生存。

解　析 除了前個單元的比較對象的用法，這個單元的句型是前個句型的進階用法，在使用 **unlike+N** 後，再以一個**形容詞子句**來修飾該名詞，豐富表達。在句型中可以看見一個形容詞子句修飾 desert lizards，子句中的語意也是正確的。主要子句中的名詞就是跟 unlike 後的名詞做比較，錯誤句中使用了 some forests 造成語法上和語意上的錯誤，而且 forests **無法執行後面動詞所表達的動作**。

檢測考點 unlike 的用法、形容詞子句、表列舉。

MP3 059

Unlike desert lizards, **which** bury themselves under the sand, some forest lizards can run onto the water for several miles to evade predators, such as snakes. Some lizards even have evolved to mimic gestures from other animals to ensure the survival.

目次 CONTENTS

Unit 1
熟悉 decrease 跟反義詞 increase 在圖表題中的用法

In 2018, agriculturalists were pleased that the price of blueberries increased nearly 25%, much greater than other fruits, but were astounded by a significant drop about the price of strawberries which decreased by 50% in the early autumn.

In 2018, agriculturalists were pleased that the price of blueberries increased nearly 25%, much greater than that of other fruits, but were astounded by a significant drop about the price of strawberries which decreased by 50% in the early autumn.

✦中　　譯✦ 在 2018 年時，農場主人對於藍莓的價格幾乎25%漲幅感到高興，這比起其他水果有著更大幅度的增加，但對於草莓價格的顯著下跌感到震驚，在早秋時下跌了50%。

✦解　　析✦ 這題要注意的考點非常多，首先時間是發生在 2018 年，所以要使用「過去式」，再來是比較級的部分，that of other fruits 的 that 是指代前面的 the price，所以未達寫作 7 分的考生要特別注意這點。錯誤句中少了 that of，the price of blueberries increased nearly 25%, much greater than that of other fruits，這也是許多考生常使用比較級時所犯的錯誤，修正這個錯誤即能迅速突破 6.5 關卡。另外要注意的是，increase 和 decrease 在句中都是當動詞的用法。

✦檢測考點✦ 圖表題中 decrease 和 increase 的用法、代名詞指代、比較級和時態。

佳句複誦

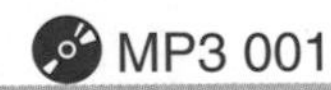

In 2018, agriculturalists were pleased that the price of blueberries **increased** nearly 25%, much greater than **that** of other fruits, but were astounded by a significant drop about the price of strawberries which **decreased** by 50% in the early autumn.

Unit 2 在各圖表題中，靈活使用 decrease 和 increase 當動詞和名詞的用法

正誤句

KEY 2

While there were a significant decrease in sales of other fruits in 2009, Best wholesalers compensated the deficit by selling other exotic vegetables, whose profit increased more than tenfold after the press release.

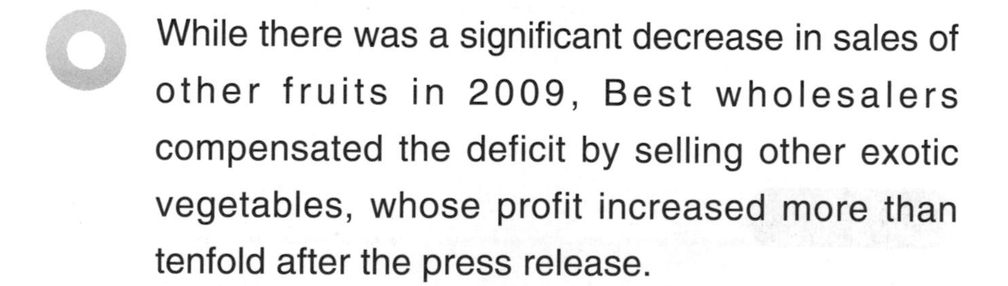

While there was a significant decrease in sales of other fruits in 2009, Best wholesalers compensated the deficit by selling other exotic vegetables, whose profit increased more than tenfold after the press release.

✦中　　譯✦ 雖然在其他水果的銷售上有顯著的跌幅，倍斯特批發商以銷售進口的蔬果來彌補赤字，進口水果的利潤在新聞發表會後就增加了 10 倍。

✦解　　析✦ 這題首先要熟悉 while 的用法，還有搭配 there is/are 的用法跟時態，there was a decrease/increase 是圖表題常用的套句，可以搭配高階形容詞修飾 increase/decrease 讓表達更清楚，另外要注意的是，這個 while 的句型，不僅是 while S+V..., S+V...，其後還多了關係代名詞子句修飾，根據語法必須要使用 whose，whose 子句裡還包含使用到 increase 當動詞的用法及跟 tenfold 的搭配。根據時態要使用 there was，錯誤句中誤用了 were。

✦檢測考點✦ While 的用法、decrease 當名詞、increase 當動詞的用法、whose 的用法。

佳句複誦

MP3 002

While there was a significant decrease in sales of other fruits, Best wholesalers compensated the deficit by selling other exotic vegetables, whose profit increased more than tenfold after the press release.

Unit 3
搭配像是 tremendous 這樣的形容詞，而成了 a tremendous decrease

正誤句

KEY 3

✗ The population of lions had tremendous increase during the great migration because of a sudden surge of wildebeests and zebras, but was dwindled to a much lower point after they had left.

○ The population of lions had a tremendous increase during the great migration because of a sudden surge of wildebeests and zebras, but was dwindled to a much lower point after they had left.

✦中　　譯✦ 獅子族群在大遷徙期間因為突然湧現的牛羚和斑馬有著巨幅的增加，但是在牠們離開後，數量降至更新低點。

✦解　　析✦ 句子的主詞是 population，主要動詞為過去式動詞 had，其後搭配了 because of，but 後使用了高階的動詞 dwindle，建議將這個搭配學起來。在錯誤句中，tremendous increase 前少了冠詞 a，在寫作時也要特別小心這些細節點。

✦檢測考點✦ Because of 的用法、but 的用法、dwindle 的用法。

佳句複誦

The **population** of lions had **a tremendous increase** during the great migration because of **a sudden surge** of wildebeests and zebras, but was dwindled to a much lower point after they had left.

Unit 4
搭配高階形容詞且把敘述具體化，例如改成 a staggering 50% decrease

正誤句

KEY 4

The population of poison dart frogs diminishing to only 2,000 in the tropical rainforest, a staggering 50% decrease from last year, and most scientists are worried that deforestation might be the direct cause for such a significant drop.

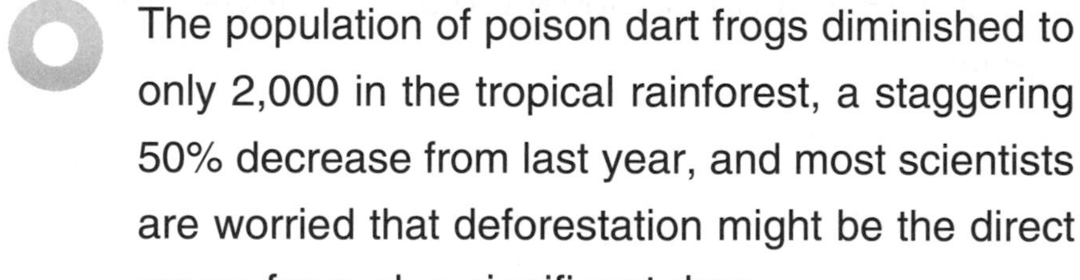

The population of poison dart frogs diminished to only 2,000 in the tropical rainforest, a staggering 50% decrease from last year, and most scientists are worried that deforestation might be the direct cause for such a significant drop.

中　　譯 在熱帶雨林中，箭毒蛙的數量降至僅剩 2000 隻，比起去年來說有顯著 50%跌幅，而大多數的科學家擔憂森林的砍伐可能是族群數量如此顯著下跌的直接原因。

解　　析 這句的主詞是 population，主要動詞是 diminished，其後加上了同位語 a staggering 50% decrease from last year 補充說明所減少了幅度，這樣可以增加句型的表達的複雜度，進而提高分數，後面更進一步說明跌幅的主因，句意表達清晰，錯誤句中使用了 diminishing，如此造成了第一個句子沒有主要動詞，所以是錯誤的，要特別小心。

檢測考點 Diminish 的用法、同位語 a staggering 50% decrease 的用法。

佳句複誦

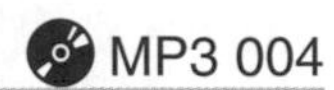

The population of poison dart frogs diminished to only 2,000 in the tropical rainforest, a staggering 50% decrease from last year, and most scientists are worried that deforestation might be **the direct cause** for such **a significant drop**.

Unit 5
學習高階圖表題「動詞」，像是使用 balloon（激增）、dwindle（減少）

KEY 5

The population of African meerkats ballooned to an unprecedented high due to a lack of predators in the area, but was later dwindled to a new low because the diminishing number of food resources, such as scorpions.

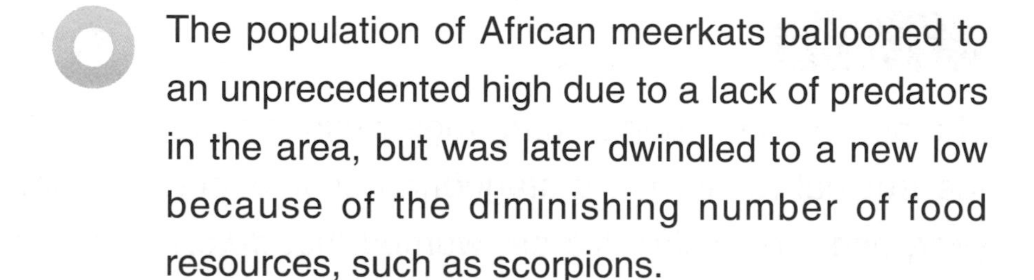

The population of African meerkats ballooned to an unprecedented high due to a lack of predators in the area, but was later dwindled to a new low because of the diminishing number of food resources, such as scorpions.

✦中　　譯✦ 由於在該地區缺乏掠食者，非洲貓鼬的族群激增至史無前例的新高，但是於稍後降至新低點，因為毒蠍類這樣的食物來源逐漸的減少。

✦解　　析✦ 這個句型中連續使用了數個高階表達的字 balloon（激增）、dwindle（減少）、diminishing（遞減的），是高分水平的句子。句子的主詞為 population，主要動詞是 ballooned，but 後的動詞為 was dwindled，也沒問題，錯誤句中使用了 because 而非 because of，because 後面必須要加上子句，故不合語法，在使用 because 和 because of 時可以多注意兩者間的差異處。

✦檢測考點✦ balloon（激增）、dwindle（減少）、diminishing（遞減的）的用法。

佳句複誦

MP3 005

The population of African meerkats ballooned to an **unprecedented** high due to a lack of predators in the area, but was later dwindled to a new low because of the diminishing number of food resources, **such as** scorpions.

Unit 6
使用高階動詞（abate）並搭配高階的副詞修飾

正誤句

KEY 6

✗ The population of octopuses abated remarkable due to illegal hunting activities and habitat changes; as a result, species which feed on them both need to find other food resources and are significantly influenced by a lack of ample food.

○ The population of octopuses abated remarkably due to illegal hunting activities and habitat changes; as a result, species which feed on them both need to find other food resources and are significantly influenced by a lack of ample food.

✦中　　譯✦ 章魚族群由於非法的獵捕活動和棲地的改變而有著顯著地減少；因此，以章魚為食的物種均需要找尋其他食物來源且受到缺乏足夠食物的大幅影響。

✦解　　析✦ 錯誤句中使用的是形容詞 remarkable，但是動詞 abated 要使用副詞修飾，所以要使用 **remarkably**，在詞跟詞搭配上可多注意些。

✦檢測考點✦ 副詞進一步修飾高階動詞的用法、abate 的用法、due to 的用法、as a result 的用法。

佳句複誦

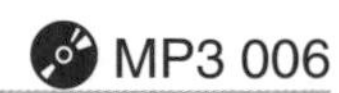

The population of octopuses abated remarkably **due to** illegal hunting activities and habitat changes; as a result, species **which** feed on them both need to find other food resources and **are significantly influenced** by a lack of ample food.

Unit 7
使用高階動詞後搭配同位語表達（例如：a staggering 500% increase from last year）

正誤句

KEY 7

The sales of 5G smartphones might bring a huge profit for multiple cellphone companies, and some even make the boldest claim that they will bring at least profit of 1 billion dollars to huge cellphone companies, a staggering 500% increase to non-5G flagship products.

The sales of 5G smartphones might bring a huge profit for multiple cellphone companies, and some even make the boldest claim that they will bring at least profit of 1 billion dollars to huge cellphone companies, a staggering 500% increase to those of non-5G flagship products.

◆中　譯◆ 5G 智慧型手機的銷售可能替眾多手機公司帶來巨額的利潤，而有些甚至明目張膽地宣稱 5G 智慧型手機會替手機大廠帶來至少十億元的利潤，這是那些非 5G 旗艦產品銷售的 500%增幅。

◆解　析◆ 錯誤句中僅使用了 non-5G flagship products，造成修飾上的錯誤，需要修正成 that of non-5G flagship products，因為是跟 The sales of 5G smartphones 做比較，所以比較對象為 the sales of non-5G flagship products，而非僅是 non-5G flagship products。

◆檢測考點◆ 同位語的用法、代名詞指代和比較級的用法。

佳句複誦

MP3 007

The sales of 5G smartphones might bring a huge profit for multiple cellphone companies, and some even make the boldest claim that they will bring at least profit of 1 billion dollars to huge cellphone companies, a staggering 500% increase to **those of** non-5G flagship products.

Unit 8
同義詞❶：單字替換

正誤句

KEY 8

Giant hornets are exceeding large predators because they are twice the size of other normal hornets, and they are also considered extremely enormous to honeybees.

Giant hornets are exceedingly large predators because they are twice the size of other normal hornets, and they are also considered extremely enormous to honeybees.

✦中　　譯✦ 巨型大黃蜂是非常大的掠食者因為牠們的體積是普通大黃蜂的兩倍，而對於蜜蜂來說，牠們也被視為是體型極大的生物。

✦解　　析✦ 這個句子中主詞為 giant hornets，主要動詞為 are，但在錯誤句中卻誤用了 exceeding large，應該修正成副詞搭配形容詞，即 exceedingly large，要特別小心這點。

✦檢測考點✦ 副詞加形容詞的搭配、twice 的用法、consider 的用法。

佳句複誦

Giant hornets are exceedingly large predators because they are **twice the size** of other normal hornets, and they are also considered extremely enormous to honeybees.

Unit 9
同義詞 ❷：使用替換的片語 / 子句

正誤句

KEY 9

Oysters are creatures that contains high levels of zinc, a chemical element that is highly relevant to growth and development for human beings, so consuming zinc-rich mollusks is essential for us.

Oysters are creatures that contain high levels of zinc, a chemical element that is highly relevant to growth and development for human beings, so consuming zinc-rich mollusks is essential for us.

✦中　　譯✦ 牡蠣含有高濃度的鋅，一種對於人類的生長和發展有高度相關性的化學物質，所以攝食富含鋅的軟體動物對我們來說是必要的。

✦解　　析✦ 這個句子中主詞為 oysters，主要動詞為 are，到這邊都沒問題，但在形容詞子句修飾時，卻使用了單數的動詞 contains，但是 creatures 為複數，所以要修正將其改為複數動詞 **contain**。還有句型中，除了形容詞子句修飾補充說明 creatures 外，還有同位語解釋 zinc，增加句子表達的複雜度，這樣的表達在雅思閱讀文章中也很常見，可以學起來。

✦檢測考點✦ 形容詞子句的用法、同位語的用法、同義字替換、so 的用法。

佳句複誦

MP3 009

Oysters are creatures **that contain** high levels of zinc, a chemical element that is highly relevant to growth and development for human beings, so consuming zinc-rich mollusks is essential for us.

Unit 10
同義詞 ❸：較進階的替換

正誤句

KEY 10

Zinc-abundant creatures, such as oysters, includes essential nutrients to growth and development for human beings, so necessity of consuming mollusks rich in essential nourishment will be good for us.

Zinc-abundant creatures, such as oysters, include essential nutrients to growth and development for human beings, so necessity of consuming mollusks rich in essential nourishment will be good for us.

✦中　　譯✦ 富含鋅的生物，例如牡蠣，涵蓋了人類生長所必需的營養素，因此攝食富含必要營養物的軟體動物對我們來說是有益處的。

✦解　　析✦ Zinc=essential nutrients，zinc-abundant creature=oysters =mollusks= mollusks rich in essential nourishment.，這個句子中包含了數個同義轉換，這些都是出題者可能在閱讀測驗中改寫跟替換的部分，可以多留意。另外要注意的是，錯誤句中，誤使用了單數動詞 includes，但主要主詞為複數 creatures。

✦檢測考點✦ 同義字轉換、表列舉 such as 的用法、形容詞子句省略的用法。

佳句複誦

MP3 010

Zinc-abundant creatures, **such as** oysters, **include** essential nutrients to growth and development for human beings, **so** necessity of consuming mollusks **rich in** essential nourishment will be good for us.

Unit 11
在圖表題作文中，數個重點之間「相似處」和「相異處」的比較

KEY 11

Similar to the behavior of their distant cousins, such as brown bears, raccoons are also omnivores, which consume swamp crabs, fruits, and vegetables, whereas the stark contrast between these two creatures are that brown bears can be formidable predators.

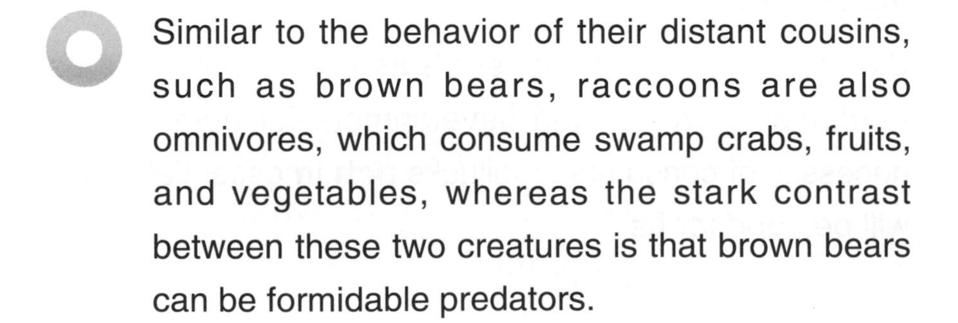

Similar to the behavior of their distant cousins, such as brown bears, raccoons are also omnivores, which consume swamp crabs, fruits, and vegetables, whereas the stark contrast between these two creatures is that brown bears can be formidable predators.

✦中　　譯✦ 浣熊，與牠們的遠親 棕熊行為相似的地方是，牠們也同樣是雜食性動物，攝食沼澤螃蟹、水果和蔬菜，而牠們兩種生物的顯著差異是，棕熊可以是令人生畏的掠食者。

✦解　　析✦ 在圖表題中，僅列出或陳述重點，對於考官來說是不夠的，要突破寫作 6.5 分，在表達這些重點時，適時的比較「相似處」和「相異處」是提高分數的關鍵。這個句子中就使用了 similar to，並搭配列舉 such as，主要句子後又加上了形容詞子句和 whereas 等是極高分的表達句。錯誤句中誤用了 are 當動詞，但是主詞 the stark contrast 中 contrast 要使用單數動詞 is 才正確。

✦檢測考點✦ Similar to 的用法、表列舉 such as 的用法、形容詞子句的用法、whereas 的用法。

佳句複誦

MP3 011

Similar to the behavior of their distant cousins, **such as** brown bears, raccoons are also omnivores, **which** consume swamp crabs, fruits, and vegetables, **whereas** the stark contrast between **these** two creatures **is** that brown bears can be formidable predators.

Unit 12
圖表題開頭的使用套句：Given is a diagram… 數個形容詞子句的省略

正誤句

KEY 12

✗ Given are two diagrams that illustrate the number of giant hornets fluctuated between 2018 and 2019, and 10 factors that influenced the population growth, conducted by Best Laboratory, an elite research center located in Taiwan.

○ Given are two diagrams that illustrate the number of giant hornets fluctuated between 2018 and 2019, and there were 10 factors that influenced the population growth, conducted by Best Laboratory, an elite research center located in Taiwan.

◆中　譯◆ 提供的是一個圖表說明大黃蜂數量在 2018 與 2019 年間的族群波動，以及 10 個影響族群成長的因素，由位於台灣的菁英研究中心，倍斯特實驗室所進行的研究。

◆解　析◆ 這個句子中使用了 Given are two diagrams that 的高分開頭，並搭配了數個形容詞子句的省略和同位語。第一個省略是 conducted 前，省略了 which was，第二個省略是在 located 前，省略了 which is，同位語的部分是 an elite research center located in Taiwan 補充說明 Best Laboratory。在錯誤句中 and 後第二個句子中少了主要動詞。

◆檢測考點◆ 圖表題高階表達句、形容詞子句省略的用法、同位語的用法。

佳句複誦

MP3 012

Given are two diagrams that illustrate the number of giant hornets fluctuated between 2018 and 2019, and there were 10 factors that influenced the population growth, **conducted** by Best Laboratory, **an elite research center located in Taiwan.**

Unit 13
圖表題中段的輔助句：It is intriguing to know that…

正誤句

KEY 13

It is intriguing to know that the successful rate of stealing a huge slice of honey from honeybees was only 35% in 2018, compared with thieving honey in 2019.

It is intriguing to know that the successful rate of stealing a huge slice of honey from honeybees was only 35% in 2018, compared with that of thieving honey in 2019.

✦中　　譯✦ 引人注意的是，在 2018 年從蜜蜂那裏成功竊取一大片蜂蜜的成功率僅只有 35%，與 2019 年的竊取成功率相比的話。

✦解　　析✦ 句子使用了圖表題常見搭配句 It is intriguing to know that，並搭配了 compared with 來比較細節點，而在錯誤句中，誤用了 compared with thieving honey in 2019，應該要修正為 compared with that of thieving honey in 2019，不然會造成比較的錯誤，因為是 2018 年的 the successful rate of stealing a huge slice of honey...和 2019 年的比較，that 代替 successful rate。

✦檢測考點✦ 圖表題常見表達句、時態、比較級、compared with 的用法。

佳句複誦

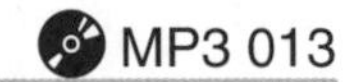

It is intriguing to know that the successful rate of stealing a huge slice of honey from honeybees was only 35% in 2018, compared with **that of** thieving honey in 2019.

Unit 14
圖表題中段的加強句 ❶：Also remarkable is the fact that...

正誤句

KEY 14

Also remarkable is the fact that bears are easily lured by the smell of honey since it has a sweet tooth, and adult bears have higher successful stealing rates because they can stand for more stings and are more persistent, according to an earlier report.

Also remarkable is the fact that bears are easily lured by the smell of honey since they have a sweet tooth, and adult bears have higher successful stealing rates because they can stand for more stings and are more persistent, according to an earlier report.

✦中　　譯✦ 也值得注意的是，熊很容易受到蜂蜜的香氣所誘惑，因為牠們嗜吃甜食，而成年的熊有較高的成功竊取率，因為牠們能夠抵抗更多的螫咬和更具毅力，根據稍早前的報導。

✦解　　析✦ 句子使用了圖表題常見搭配句 Also remarkable is the fact that，其後使用了 since 等句型豐富句式，而在錯誤句中發生了代名詞指代的錯誤，since 後誤用了 it has，描述有 sweet tooth 的是指前面句子主詞 bears，所以應該要使用 they，且動詞要改為 have。

✦檢測考點✦ 圖表題常見表達句、被動語態、慣用語、比較級的用法。

佳句複誦

MP3 014

Also remarkable is the fact that bears **are easily lured by** the smell of honey since they have a sweet tooth, and adult bears have higher successful stealing rates because they can stand for more stings and are more persistent, according to an earlier report.

Unit 15 圖表題中段的加強句 ❷：From the information provided⋯

正誤句

KEY 15

From the information provided, younger bears still need more guidance by mother bears in various circumstances because there is still too many things for them to learn, and stealing honey and catching salmons is two of the necessary skills for them.

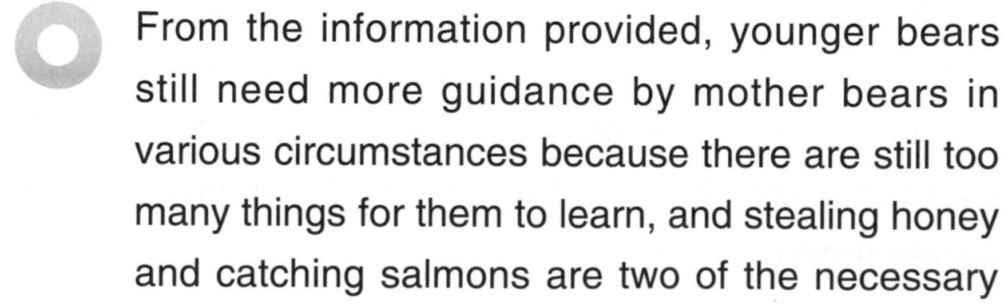

From the information provided, younger bears still need more guidance by mother bears in various circumstances because there are still too many things for them to learn, and stealing honey and catching salmons are two of the necessary skills for them.

✦中　　譯✦ 從所提供的資料顯示，在不同情況中，較年輕的熊仍需要母熊的指導因為還有許多事情是牠們需要學習的，而偷取蜂蜜和捕獲鮭魚對於牠們來說是其中兩項必要的技能。

✦解　　析✦ 句子使用了圖表題常見搭配句 From the information provided，其後也使用了數個句式增進表達。在錯誤句中，there 的句型誤用了 is，但是 too many things 為複數，還有另一個錯誤發生在 and 後的動名詞當主詞的句型中，當中有兩個動名詞當主詞，所以動詞要使用 **are** 才是對的。

✦檢測考點✦ 圖表題常見表達句、because、there are、two of 的用法。

佳句複誦

From the information provided, younger bears still need more guidance by mother bears in various circumstances **because** there are still too many things for them to learn, and stealing honey and catching salmons **are** two of the necessary skills for them.

Unit 16
使用複雜的句式解釋名詞：形容詞子句和同位語

正誤句

KEY 16

Honeycombs, wax structures that can stockpile honey and pollens, is unique designs and can be used as places to nurture larvae, offspring of bees that will benefit the feeder by secreting chemical substances that is essential for growth of bees.

Honeycombs, wax structures that can stockpile honey and pollens, are unique designs and can be used as places to nurture larvae, offspring of bees that will benefit the feeder by secreting chemical substances that are essential for growth of bees.

✦中　　譯✦ 蜂巢為一蠟狀結構能儲藏蜂蜜和花粉，是個獨特的設計且能用於培育蜜蜂幼蟲，幼蟲為蜜蜂後代，其對餵食者的益處是會藉由分泌對蜜蜂成長必要的化學物質反饋。

✦解　　析✦ 主詞 Honeycombs 後搭配了同位語補述，在錯誤句中，卻誤用了動詞時態 is，應該更正為複數，另外，在 larvae 後也使用了同位語的表達，豐富了句式，但在 chemical substances that 後也誤用了 is 應該更正為 are，因為 substances 為複數。

✦檢測考點✦ 同位語的用法、形容詞子句的用法、慣用語、單複數。

佳句複誦

Honeycombs, **wax structures that** can stockpile honey and pollens, are unique designs and **can be used as** places to nurture larvae, **offspring of bees that** will benefit the feeder by secreting chemical substances **that are** essential for growth of bees.

Unit 17
圖表題「倍數」的用法加比較級

正誤句

KEY 17

✗ Despite the fact that a significant decline of 25.5% in sales, the sales of rare fruits eventually made a comeback and had a tenfold increase in domestic markets, much greater than those of international markets.

○ Despite a significant decline of 25.5% in sales, the sales of rare fruits eventually made a comeback and had a tenfold increase in domestic markets, much greater than those of international markets.

✦中　　譯✦ 儘管在銷售上有著 25.5%的顯著跌幅，罕見水果的銷售最終起死回生，且在國內市場的銷售有著 10 倍增幅，銷售比起那些國際市場更佳。

✦解　　析✦ 句子一開始就很具體的表達，並非僅使用 a decline，而是 a significant decline of 25.5% in sales，despite 後面加名詞或名詞片語，而如果後面要加的是子句則須使用 despite the fact that，錯誤句中誤用了 despite the fact that。在後面比較級句型中也要注意 those 指的是前面的 sales，所以是 the sales of rare fruits in domestic markets 和 the sales of rare fruits in international markets 做比較。

✦檢測考點✦ Despite 的用法、慣用語、倍數的用法、比較級的用法。

佳句複誦

Despite a significant decline of 25.5% in sales, the sales of rare fruits eventually made a comeback and had a tenfold increase in domestic markets, much greater than those of international markets.

Unit 18
「One of⋯」的句型，of 後加複數名詞且主要動詞為單數

正誤句

KEY 18

One of the biggest threats to desert chameleons are zebra snakes, which are far more intelligent and nimbler. The zebra snake in sight awaits outside the labyrinth of shrubs, astounding its prey, the unintelligent chameleon.

One of the biggest threats to desert chameleons is zebra snakes, which are far more intelligent and nimbler. The zebra snake in sight awaits outside the labyrinth of shrubs, astounding its prey, the unintelligent chameleon.

✦中　　譯✦ 對沙漠變色龍來說其中一個最大的威脅是斑馬蛇，比其更為聰明且敏捷。視線中的斑馬蛇在灌木叢迷宮外等著，令其獵物愚蠢的變色龍感到大吃一驚。

✦解　　析✦ 使用「One of...」的句型，of 後加**複數**名詞且主要動詞為單數，但在錯誤句中卻誤用了 are。另外，形容詞子句中也要用複數動詞，因為 snakes 為複數。句型中還有使用了同位語的部分，補充說明 prey。在代名詞指代的部分，要注意是 astounding **its** prey，its 指的是前面提到的 The zebra snake。

✦檢測考點✦ 「One of…」的句型、形容詞子句的用法、同位語的用法、代名詞指代。

佳句複誦

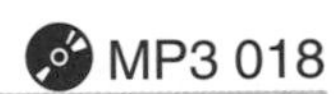

One of the biggest threats to desert chameleons is zebra snakes, which are far more intelligent and nimbler. The zebra snake in sight awaits outside the labyrinth of shrubs, astounding **its** prey**, the unintelligent chameleon**.

Unit 19
「名詞片語」當主詞時的單複數❶：單數

正誤句

KEY 19

✗ The attack of the octopus are considered phenomenal and fearsome because octopuses normally cannot take down prey of such heavy weight. On rare occasions, you get to witness the gigantic octopus surprisingly attacks a great white shark.

○ The attack of the octopus is considered phenomenal and fearsome because octopuses normally cannot take down prey of such heavy weight. On rare occasions, you get to witness the gigantic octopus surprisingly attacks a great white shark.

中　譯　章魚的攻擊被視為是非凡且令人生畏的，因為章魚通常無法擊倒體積如此沉重的獵物。在罕見情況下，你能夠目睹巨型章魚出人意外地攻擊大白鯊。

解　析　首句的主詞為 attack，主要動詞為 is considered，其後加了 because 子句，子句內主詞為 octopuses，主要動詞為 take。錯誤句的地方在 The attack of the octopus are considered phenomenal and fearsome because octopuses normally cannot take down prey of such heavy weight.，主要動詞的地方要改成 is，才合乎語法。

檢測考點　Consider 的用法、「**名詞**片語」當主詞時的單複數、because 的用法。

佳句複誦

MP3 019

The attack of the octopus **is considered** phenomenal and fearsome **because** octopuses normally cannot take down prey of such heavy weight. On rare occasions, you get to witness the gigantic octopus **surprisingly attacks** a great white shark.

Unit 20
「名詞片語」當主詞時的單複數❷：複數

正誤句

KEY 20

The emotions of the male tiger are easily predicted through observing his behavior and patterns of the day. When there is an intruder, the male tiger may seem agitate and guard, fearing the unpleasant newcomer might take his throne.

The emotions of the male tiger are easily predicted through observing his behavior and patterns of the day. When there is an intruder, the male tiger may seem agitated and guarded, fearing the unpleasant newcomer might take his throne.

✦中　　譯✦ 透過觀察牠的行為和每日的生活方式，雄性老虎的情緒是易於預測的。當有闖入者來訪，雄性老虎可能表現得躁動且警惕的，擔憂這個新到訪的不速之客可能會奪取他的王位。

✦解　　析✦ 首句的主詞為 emotions，動詞為 are predicted。次句為 when 引導的副詞子句，子句中為 there is 的句型，主要子句中的動詞為 may seem。錯誤的地方在 When there is an intruder, the male tiger may seem agitate and guard, fearing the unpleasant newcomer might take his throne.，seem 後方要使用**形容詞**當補語，所以 agitate 要改正成 agitated，guard 要改成 guarded 才合乎語法。

✦檢測考點✦ 「**名詞**片語」當主詞時的單複數、through 的用法、when 的用法、seem 的用法。

佳句複誦

MP3 020

The emotions of the male tiger **are** easily predicted **through** observing his behavior and patterns of the day. **When** there is an intruder, the male tiger may **seem** agitated and guarded, fearing the unpleasant newcomer might take his throne.

Unit 21
「名詞片語」當主詞時的單複數❸：所有格形式's

KEY 21

Penguins' inability to defend themselves against the attack of the sea lion can result in getting tore up while alive, but if they are agile enough to swiftly swim in open sea, the chance to make it to the adulthood is highly likely.

Penguins' inability to defend themselves against the attack of the sea lion can result in getting tore up while alive, but if they are agile enough to swiftly swim in open sea, the chance to make it to the adulthood is highly likely.

✦中　　譯✦ 企鵝無法防衛自我抵禦海獅的攻擊可能會導致其活生生地被撕裂掉，但是如果牠們靈敏到以飛快的速度游至開放式海洋的話，活至成年的機會是相當高的。

✦解　　析✦ 首句的主詞為 inability，themselves 指代 penguins，句中的動詞為 can result，result in 的 in 後加上動名詞。錯誤的地方在 **but if it is agile enough to swiftly swim in open sea, the chance to make it to the adulthood is highly likely.**，if 子句中的 **it is** 要改成 **they are** 才符合語法。

✦檢測考點✦ 「**名詞**片語」當主詞時的單複數、but 的用法、if 的用法。

佳句複誦

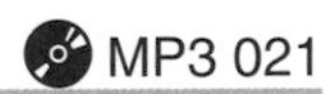

Penguins' inability to defend themselves against the attack of the sea lion can **result in** getting tore up while alive, **but if they are** agile enough to swiftly swim in open sea, the chance to make it to the adulthood is highly likely.

Unit 22
動名詞當主詞時，主要動詞要用單數動詞

正誤句

KEY 22

Remaining impervious to any disturbance in the tropical rainforests are not easy because there are too many creatures in there. Insects which are readily perturbed by natural forces, such as rain and wind, can be vulnerable to attack by their predators.

Remaining impervious to any disturbance in the tropical rainforests is not easy because there are too many creatures in there. Insects which are readily perturbed by natural forces, such as rain and wind, can be vulnerable to attack by their predators.

✦中　　譯✦ 面對熱帶雨林中的任何擾動都能不為所動是件不容易的事，因為有太多生物存在其中。越易受到自然力量，例如雨和風擾動者，越易於受到掠食者的攻擊。

✦解　　析✦ 儘管動詞前的敘述是名詞片語（the tropical rainforests）且是複數，但是這個句型是動名詞當主詞，根據語法動名詞當主詞時，主要動詞要用單數動詞，所以要使用單數動詞 is（而非 are），要小心別被**複數名詞**干擾到。

另外要注意的是句子的第二句，修飾 insects 的關係代名詞為 which。

✦檢測考點✦ 動名詞當主詞的用法、形容詞子句的用法、表列舉的用法。

佳句複誦

Remaining impervious to any disturbance in the tropical rainforests is not easy because there are too many creatures in there. Insects **which are** readily perturbed by natural forces, **such as** rain and wind, can be vulnerable to attack by their predators.

Unit 23
「兩個」動名詞當主詞時，主要動詞要用複數動詞

正誤句

KEY 23

✗ Finding the right place to ambush and evaluating the time to launch an attack is highly relevant to the success rate of hunting large prey. Sometimes attacking involves avoiding the horn of the rhino or the kick of the giraffe, so that predators can remain unharmed during the attack.

○ Finding the right place to ambush and evaluating the time to launch an attack are highly relevant to the success rate of hunting large prey. Sometimes attacking involves avoiding the horn of the rhino or the kick of the giraffe, so that predators can remain unharmed during the attack.

✦中　　譯✦ 找尋正確的位置埋伏和評估發動攻擊的時間與獵捕大型獵物的成功機率是高度相關的。有時候，攻擊包含避免被犀牛或是長頸鹿的踢擊，如此一來掠食者就能在攻擊期間毫髮無傷。

✦解　　析✦ 句型中使用了兩個動名詞當主詞的描述 **Finding**（Ving 1） the right place to ambush and **evaluating**（Ving 2） the time to launch an attack are highly relevant to the success rate of hunting large prey.，在錯誤句中卻使用了單數動詞 is，要改為 are。

✦檢測考點✦ 動名詞當主詞的用法（**複數動詞**）、so 的用法、remain 的用法。

佳句複誦

Finding the right place to ambush and evaluating the time to launch an attack are highly relevant to the success rate of hunting large prey. Sometimes attacking **involves** avoiding the horn of the rhino or the kick of the giraffe, so that predators can remain unharmed during the attack.

Unit 24
若是於過去發生的狀態，動名詞當主詞時，要用「過去式」單數動詞

正誤句

KEY 24

The elephant was badly tortured because it did want not to obey the instructions given by the trainer of the Animal Circus. Attending the funeral of the elephant in Animal Shelter is one of the horrible experiences in Doctor Mark's life.

The elephant was badly tortured because it did want not to obey the instructions given by the trainer of the Animal Circus. Attending the funeral of the elephant in Animal Shelter was one of the horrible experiences in Doctor Mark's life.

✦中　譯✦ 那頭大象因為其不想要遵從動物馬戲團訓練者所發出的指示而受到嚴重地折磨。在動物庇護所中參加大象的葬禮是馬克醫生生命中的一個可怕的經驗。

✦解　析✦ 在這個句子中，儘管沒有出現相關的時間或日期表明（提醒）這是在過去的時間所發生的，但是**「參加葬禮」**是過去發生的事要用過去式。另外要掌握的是，動名詞當主詞時，動詞要用第三人稱單數，所以綜合這兩點，可以得知要使用的動詞是第三人稱單數且是過去時態的動詞 was。

✦檢測考點✦ 被動語態、because 的用法、動名詞當主詞的用法（**過去式動詞**）。

佳句複誦

The elephant **was badly tortured** because it did want not to obey the instructions given by the trainer of the Animal Circus. Attending the funeral of the elephant in Animal Shelter was one of the horrible experiences in Doctor Mark's life.

Unit 25
動名詞當主詞 because 引導的副詞子句

正誤句

KEY 25

Roaming on the savanna in South Africa are very precarious because there are multiple predators, such as lions, hyenas, and cheetahs, hungry for the meal. Tourists traveling there should be very vigilant and stay in the car to ensure their safety.

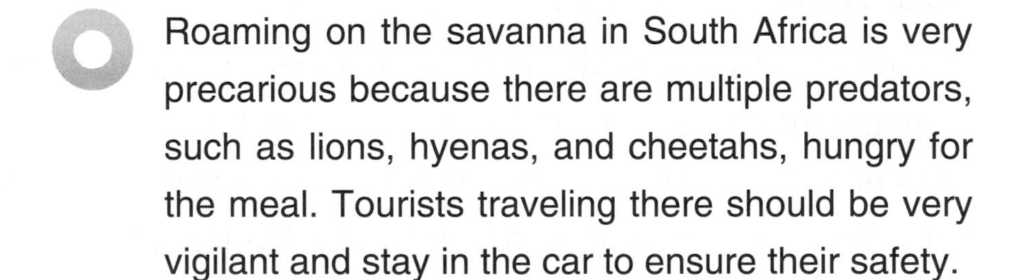

Roaming on the savanna in South Africa is very precarious because there are multiple predators, such as lions, hyenas, and cheetahs, hungry for the meal. Tourists traveling there should be very vigilant and stay in the car to ensure their safety.

✦中　　譯✦ 漫步在南非大草原上是非常危險的，因為那兒有多樣的掠食者，例如獅子、土狼和獵豹，飢腸轆轆地等著大餐降臨。旅行此地的觀光客應該要非常警惕且待在車上以確保安全。

✦解　　析✦ 錯誤句中誤用了複數動詞 are，但是動名詞當主詞時要使用單數動詞，所以要修正為 is。在表列舉後方，hungry 前為形容詞子句的省略，前面省略了 which are，讓句子更簡潔。另一個有省略的地方是，tourists traveling，traveling 為 who travel 變成的。

✦檢測考點✦ 動名詞當主詞 because、表列舉的用法。

佳句複誦

Roaming on the savanna in South Africa is very precarious because there are multiple predators, such as lions, hyenas, and cheetahs, hungry for the meal. Tourists traveling there **should be** very vigilant and stay in the car to ensure their safety.

Unit 26
動名詞細節部分：「Ing- 形式」修飾的複數名詞主詞和動名詞的區隔

正誤句

KEY 26

Developing lion cubs is in desperate need of the protection from both adult lions (female and male) since they are too vulnerable to any impending danger. Playing is also important for these cubs to build muscle strength and necessary hunting skills for later survival.

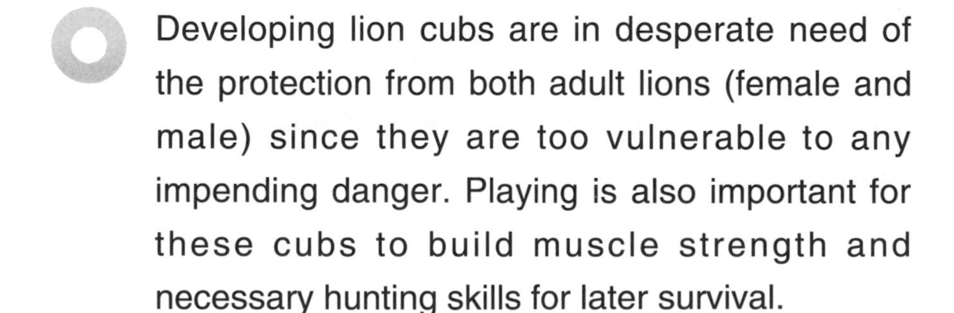

Developing lion cubs are in desperate need of the protection from both adult lions (female and male) since they are too vulnerable to any impending danger. Playing is also important for these cubs to build muscle strength and necessary hunting skills for later survival.

中 譯 發育中的獅子幼獸急迫切需要成年獅子（雌性或雄性獅子）的保護，因為任何迫在眉睫的危險都使牠們易受到攻擊。對於稍後生存，玩耍對於這些幼獸來說也是重要的，此舉能使得其強化肌肉力量和必需的狩獵技巧。

解 析 這題很重要的部分是「Ing-形式」修飾的複數名詞主詞和動名詞的區隔。尤其在選擇題很容易看太快誤判是動名詞當主詞，但其實 Ving 僅是在修飾複數名詞，所以錯誤句需要修正為 Developing lion cubs **are**。

檢測考點 「**Ing-形式**」修飾的複數名詞主詞和動名詞的區隔、since 的用法。

佳句複誦

MP3 026

Developing lion cubs are in desperate need of the protection from both adult lions (female and male) since they are too vulnerable to any **impending** danger. Playing **is** also important for these cubs to build muscle strength and necessary hunting skills for later survival.

Unit 27
動名詞常見慣用語：be devoted to

KEY 27

Female lions just giving birth to newborn cubs are devoting more of their time to hunting activities. They have to find a concealed place, hiding those cubs and nurturing them from time to time.

Female lions just giving birth to newborn cubs are devoting less of their time to hunting activities. They have to find a concealed place, hiding those cubs and nurturing them from time to time.

✦中　　譯✦ 剛生下新生幼獸的雌性獅子較少將牠們的時間致力於獵捕活動上。牠們必須要找到一個隱匿的地方，來藏匿那些幼獸且偶爾撫育牠們。

✦解　　析✦ 這個句型中介紹了「動名詞常見慣用語」中的 be devoted to，be devoted to=devoted oneself to 其後加 N/Ving。句中的主詞為 lions，主要動詞為 are。錯誤的地方在句中的 more，Female lions just giving birth to newborn cubs are devoting more of their time to hunting activities.，使用 more 雖合乎語法，但於語意上不合，因為剛生小獅子後，母獅花費在獅群狩獵的時間就會因為小獅子的出生而減少了。

✦檢測考點✦ 形容詞子句省略的用法、動名詞常見慣用語（devote）、have to 的用法。

佳句複誦

MP3 027

Female lions just giving birth to newborn cubs are **devoting** less of their time **to** hunting activities. They **have to** find a concealed place, hiding those cubs and nurturing them from time to time.

Unit 28
不定詞當主詞時，主要動詞要用單數動詞

正誤句

KEY 28

To take down such a giant giraffe require multiple experienced female lions to work in unison. The giraffe can run pretty fast and its height prevents itself from getting grasped by lions.

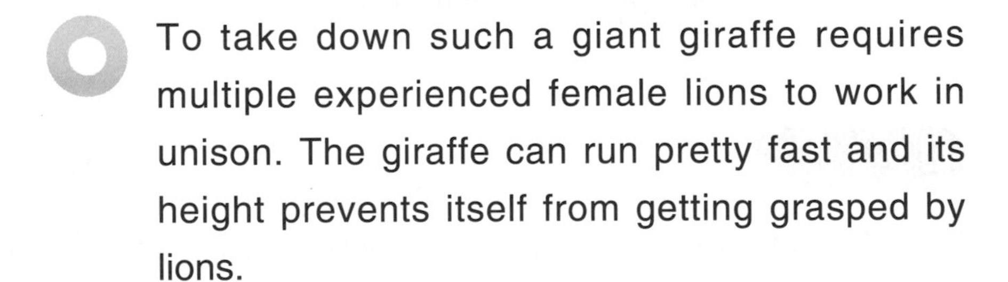

To take down such a giant giraffe requires multiple experienced female lions to work in unison. The giraffe can run pretty fast and its height prevents itself from getting grasped by lions.

✦中　　譯✦ 要擊倒如此大型的長頸鹿需要多數有經驗的雌性獅子同一協力攻擊。長頸鹿可能跑的非常快，且其身高讓長頸鹿本身免於被獅子抓到。

✦解　　析✦ 不定詞當主詞時要用單數動詞，所以要將錯誤句中的動詞時態修正為 requires。另外要注意的是，代名詞指代的部份，its height 中的 its 指的是 giraffe，而 prevent itself 中 itself 也指的是 giraffe，這些都是相關的，在寫作時要特別注意就是了。

✦檢測考點✦ 不定詞當主詞時要用單數動詞、代名詞指代的用法、prevent from 的用法。

佳句複誦

To take down such a giant giraffe requires multiple experienced female lions to work in unison. The giraffe can run pretty fast and its height prevents itself from getting grasped by lions.

Unit 29
不定詞 To+V..., ...S+V 的句型

KEY 29

To protect themselves from getting spotted by larger birds, the male chameleon uses its instinct to change its appearance. Sometimes coloration will not do the magic and it unanticipatedly gets devoured by a large crane.

To protect itself from getting spotted by larger birds, the male chameleon uses its instinct to change its appearance. Sometimes coloration will not do the magic and it unanticipatedly gets devoured by a large crane.

✦中　　譯✦ 要免於被較大型的鳥類察覺，這隻雄性的變色龍使用牠的本能來變換外貌。有時候顏色變換無法發揮其魔法效果，變色龍出乎意料之外地被大型鶴吞下肚。

✦解　　析✦ 這個句型中介紹了【不定詞 To+V..., ...S+V 的句型】，句中的主要主詞為 chameleon，並且使用了單數動詞 uses。錯誤的地方在 To protect themselves from getting spotted by larger birds, the male chameleon uses its instinct to change its appearance，to protect 後的反身代名詞指的是 chameleon，故要將 themselves 改成 itself 才是正確的用法。

✦檢測考點✦ 不定詞 To+V,...S+V 的句型、protect from 的用法、代名詞指代的用法。

佳句複誦

MP3 029

To protect itself from getting spotted by larger birds, the male chameleon uses its instinct to change its appearance. Sometimes coloration will not do the magic and it unanticipatedly gets devoured by a large crane.

Unit 30
不定詞常見慣用語：intend to+V

正誤句

KEY 30

The head of the female lion intends initiating the attack, and the next thing you witness is her teammates rushing towards the prey in five different directions. The move can astonish the unsuspecting prey, and luckily, geography works in favor of the female lions.

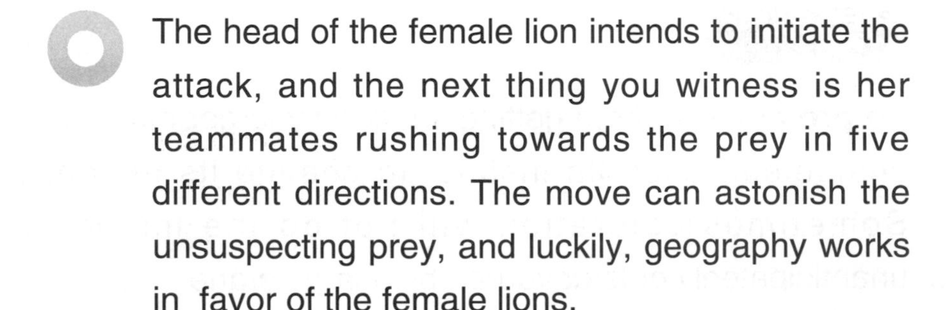

The head of the female lion intends to initiate the attack, and the next thing you witness is her teammates rushing towards the prey in five different directions. The move can astonish the unsuspecting prey, and luckily, geography works in favor of the female lions.

✦中　　譯✦ 雌性獅子的首領意圖發動攻擊，接下來你目睹了牠的團隊從五個不同的方位衝向獵物。此舉可能會驚動毫無戒心的獵物，而幸運的是，地勢有利於雌性獅子這方。

✦解　　析✦ 這題考的是對於不定詞的常見慣用語的掌握，不定詞後面要加 to+V 的形式，intend 後面即是，但是在錯誤句中，intend 後卻是 initiating，要修正為 intends to initiate the attack。另外要注意的是，句子中的主詞是 head，所以主要動詞要用單數形式即 intends。

✦檢測考點✦ 不定詞常見慣用語（intend to）、其他慣用語的用法。

佳句複誦

MP3 030

The head of the female lion intends **to initiate** the attack, and the next thing you witness is her teammates rushing towards the prey in five different directions. The move can astonish the unsuspecting prey, and luckily, geography works in favor of the female lions.

Unit 31
對等連接詞連接兩個句子，「第二個」動詞的時態使用錯誤

正誤句

KEY 31

One of the female lions manages to get rid of a clan of hyenas, but still get threatened and trapped on the steep cliff where there are no escapes. All of a sudden, relief forces arrive there, trying to drive away hateful hyenas.

One of the female lions manages to get rid of a clan of hyenas, but still gets threatened and trapped on the steep cliff where there are no escapes. All of a sudden, relief forces arrive there, trying to drive away hateful hyenas.

✦中　　譯✦ 其中一隻雌性獅子設法要擺脱一群土狼，但是仍受到威脅且被困在陡峭的懸崖上，無處可逃避。突然之間，援軍到來，試圖趕走可憎的土狼們。

✦解　　析✦ 這個句型中介紹了對等連接詞的用法，非母語的學習者常在對等連接詞後誤用了動詞時態，某部分是因為可能離原來的主詞較遠，故造成「時態」使用上的錯誤。句型中錯誤的地方在 One of the female lions manages to get rid of a clan of hyenas, but still get threatened...，get 要改成 gets 才合乎語法。

✦檢測考點✦ One of 的用法、修飾語、時態、where 的用法。

佳句複誦

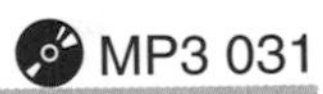

One of the female lions **manages** to get rid of **a clan of** hyenas, but still gets threatened and trapped on the steep cliff where there are no escapes. All of a sudden, relief forces arrive there, trying to drive away hateful hyenas.

Unit 32
主動詞一致：較複雜的句型 ❶

正誤句

KEY 32

One of the distinct difference between intelligence of octopuses and that of other crabs lie in octopuses' ability in tool use and many others to prevent themselves from getting captured by their predators.

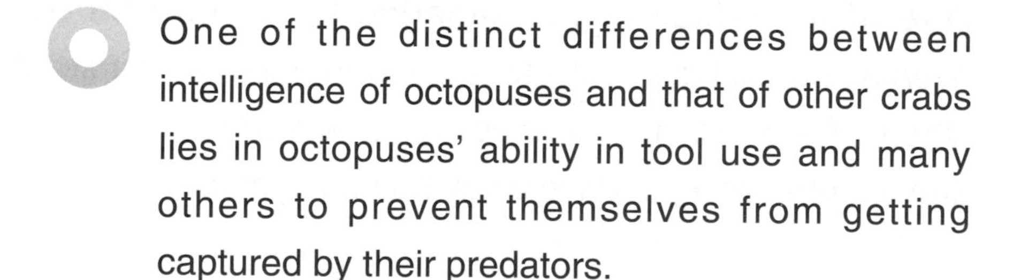

One of the distinct differences between intelligence of octopuses and that of other crabs lies in octopuses' ability in tool use and many others to prevent themselves from getting captured by their predators.

中　譯　章魚的智力和其他螃蟹的智力特別不同之處在於章魚在工具使用上的能力和許多其他的能力可以避免被其掠食者捕獲。

解　析　這題包含了 One of 的用法所以 distinct 後要加複數，在錯誤句中卻使用了單數 difference，還有需要注意的部分是主要動詞要使用單數，所以要將 lie 改成 lies。還有一個比較需要注意且常用錯的是，關於 that 的部分，這個句子中使用的蠻好的，在第二個表達 intelligence of…時，使用了 that 取代 intelligence 避免重複，如果是複數形式的名詞，則就要用 those of...要特別注意。

檢測考點　One of 的用法、代名詞指代、prevent from 的用法。

佳句複誦

One of the distinct differences between intelligence of octopuses and **that** of other crabs **lies** in octopuses' ability in tool use and many others to prevent themselves from getting captured by their predators.

Unit 33
主動詞一致：較複雜的句型 ❷

正誤句

KEY 33

✖ African lions, belligerent and skillful predators that consume herbivores, such as zebras, elephants, giraffes, rhinos, and many others, has almost no threats in the region. They might sometimes have a dispute with their neighbors, the Nile crocodiles.

○ African lions, belligerent and skillful predators that consume herbivores, such as zebras, elephants, giraffes, rhinos, and many others, have almost no threats in the region. They might sometimes have a dispute with their neighbors, the Nile crocodiles.

✦中　　譯✦ 非洲獅子是好戰且巧妙的掠食者，牠善於攝食草食性動物，例如斑馬、大象、長頸鹿、犀牛和許多其他的動物，在這個地區沒有任何的威脅。牠們有時候可能會與牠們的鄰居，尼羅河鱷魚起爭執。

✦解　　析✦ 這個句型介紹了主動詞一致中較複雜的句型，句中主詞為 lions，其後使用了同位語補充解釋 lions，其後還加上了表列舉的項目，錯誤的地方在動詞時態上的使用，African lions, belligerent and skillful predators that consume herbivores, such as zebras, elephants, giraffes, rhinos, and many others, has almost no threats in the region.，要將 has 改成 have 才合乎語法。

✦檢測考點✦ 動詞單複數、表列舉、同位語。

佳句複誦

African lions, belligerent and skillful predators that consume herbivores, such as zebras, elephants, giraffes, rhinos, and many others, have almost no threats in the region. They might sometimes have a dispute with their neighbors, the Nile crocodiles.

Unit 34
平行對稱 ❶：數個動詞的連接和對等

正誤句

KEY 34

Tourists visiting to wild Africa would have to know the dangerous creatures, avoiding any physical contact with wild animals, control the urge to photograph a click-bait picture, and smuggle illicit animal products.

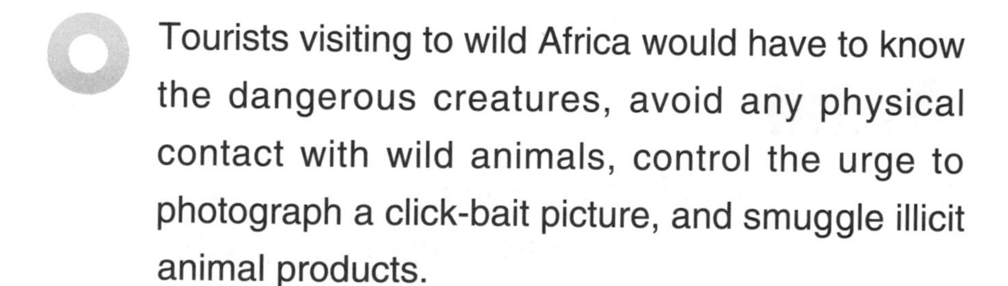

Tourists visiting to wild Africa would have to know the dangerous creatures, avoid any physical contact with wild animals, control the urge to photograph a click-bait picture, and smuggle illicit animal products.

◆中　　譯◆ 拜訪野生非洲的觀光客必須知道危險的生物，避免任何與野生動物的肢體接觸、控制拍攝「誘餌式點讚」照片的衝動和走私違法的動物產品。

◆解　　析◆ 這個句子中主要主詞為 tourists，visiting 為 who visit 的省略，而主要的動詞為 would have，不過這個句子的重點為平行對稱，所以必須要是 4 個原形動詞，to **know** the dangerous creatures, **avoid** any physical contact with wild animals, **control** the urge to photograph a click-bait picture, and **smuggle** illicit…粗體字的部分即是 V1-V4。錯誤句誤使用 avoiding。

◆檢測考點◆ 形容詞子句省略、平行對稱；**動詞**的連接、慣用語。

佳句複誦

Tourists visiting to wild Africa would have to **know** the dangerous creatures, **avoid** any physical contact with wild animals, **control** the urge to photograph a click-bait picture, and **smuggle** illicit animal products.

Unit 35
平行對稱 ❷：詞性對等－名詞

正誤句

KEY 35

The potential dangers for forest chameleons include flying ravens, venomous snakes, and gigantic. Predators consuming forest chameleons keep their numbers in check so that there is actually a balance in the forest.

The potential dangers for forest chameleons include flying ravens, venomous snakes, and gigantic cranes. Predators consuming forest chameleons keep their numbers in check so that there is actually a balance in the forest.

✦中　譯✦ 對於森林變色龍來說，潛在的危險包含了翱翔的大烏鴉、毒蛇和巨型鶴。掠食者掠食森林變色龍使得牠們的數量維持恆定，如此一來就可以維持森林裡的實際平衡。

✦解　析✦ 這個句型中介紹了平行對稱：詞性對等**－名詞**，看首句主要主詞為 dangers，主要動詞為 include，include 後表列舉的項目，可以看出其規律性「形容詞+名詞」的搭配。錯誤的地方在 The potential dangers for forest chameleons include flying ravens【**N1**】, venomous snakes【**N2**】, and gigantic.，缺少了【N3】，使得句子不合乎語法。

✦檢測考點✦ 表列舉、平行對稱：詞性對等**－名詞**、形容詞子句省略。

佳句複誦

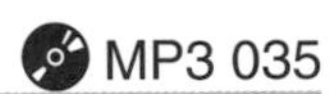
MP3 035

The potential dangers for forest chameleons **include flying ravens**, **venomous snakes**, and **gigantic cranes**. Predators consuming forest chameleons keep their numbers in check so that there is actually a balance in the forest.

Unit 36
平行對稱❸：詞性對等－形容詞

正誤句

KEY 36

✗ Visitors are astounded by the beauty of peacocks in India. Although comments about them may vary, most would say they are docile, beauty, and charming. In fiction, the galls of peacocks are served as powerful venom and can kill people in a second.

○ Visitors are astounded by the beauty of peacocks in India. Although comments about them may vary, most would say they are docile, beautiful, and charming. In fiction, the galls of peacocks are served as powerful venom and can kill people in a second.

中　譯 在印度，拜訪者因孔雀的美麗為之震驚。儘管關於孔雀的評論可能不同，大多數的人可能會將牠們評論為溫馴、美麗和有魅力的。在小說中，孔雀膽卻被充當成強而有力的毒素且能於幾秒內殺死人。

解　析 這句中也是在檢測考生對於平行對稱的掌握。在 most would say they are **docile**, **beautiful**, and **charming**.中必須是三個對等的形容詞，而在錯誤句中卻誤用了 beauty，造成了不對等的，所以要將其改成形容詞。

檢測考點 平行對稱：詞性對等–**形容詞**、被動語態、although 的用法。

佳句複誦

MP3 036

Visitors **are astounded by** the beauty of peacocks in India. Although comments about them may vary, most would say they **are** docile, beautiful, and charming. In fiction, the galls of peacocks are served as powerful venom and can kill people in a second.

Unit 37
平行對稱 ❹：名詞子句的對等

KEY 37

It is widely known in the desert that animals regulate the water loss and how advanced animals' defense mechanism against desert heat eventually determine the survival rate. Fennecs have evolved to have two huge ears that dissipate desert heat.

It is widely known in the desert that how well animals regulate the water loss and how advanced animals' defense mechanism against desert heat eventually determine the survival rate. Fennecs have evolved to have two huge ears that dissipate desert heat.

✦中　　譯✦ 在沙漠中廣為人知的是動物如何控管水分的流失和進階的動物防衛機制以抵禦沙漠的熱度，最終決定著生存率。耳廓狐已演化出具有兩隻大耳朵，用於驅散沙漠的熱度。

✦解　　析✦ 這個句型介紹了較複雜的平行對稱，平行對稱：**名詞子句**的對等，常見的是其中一個平行對稱的對象，僅是名詞片語或句子，但並非名詞子句，故造成了不對稱的情況出現。所以在 It is widely known in the desert that **animals regulate the water loss** and how advanced animals' defense mechanism against desert heat eventually determine the survival rate，animals 前面要加上 how well 才合乎語法。.

✦檢測考點✦ 平行對稱：**名詞子句**的對等、時態、形容詞子句的用法。

佳句複誦

It is widely known in the desert that how well animals regulate the water loss **and** how advanced animals' defense mechanism against desert heat eventually determine the survival rate. Fennecs have evolved to have two huge ears that dissipate desert heat.

Unit 38
平行對稱 ❺：形容詞子句的對等

正誤句

KEY 38

The potential dangers for forest chameleons include flying ravens, which launch a surprise attack, venomous snakes, whose toxin paralyzes their body, and gigantic cranes, devour them through air foray.

The potential dangers for forest chameleons include flying ravens, which launch a surprise attack, venomous snakes, whose toxin paralyzes their body, and gigantic cranes, which devour them through air foray.

中　　譯 對於森林變色龍來說潛在的危險包含了發動突擊的飛翔烏鴉、有著癱瘓其身體毒素的毒蛇，以及透過空襲吞噬牠們的巨型鶴。

解　　析 這個句子中的主要主詞是 **dangers**，而主要動詞是 **include**，到這邊都沒問題，接著看表列舉的三種動物都分別進一步有形容詞子句來修飾，是更進階的句子表達。所以在這題，很明顯的是要檢測形容詞子句的對等，在錯誤句中，**devour** 前卻無故省略掉了 **devour** 造成了不對等的關係，要將其修正。

檢測考點 平行對稱：**形容詞子句**的對等、表列舉。

佳句複誦

MP3 038

The potential dangers for forest chameleons **include** flying ravens, which launch a surprise attack, venomous snakes, whose toxin paralyzes their body, and gigantic cranes, which devour them through air foray.

Unit 39
平行對稱 ❻：時態一致

正誤句

KEY 39

Marine biologists investigating the behavior of octopuses in the Pacific a few years ago have now reached a consensus about the intelligence of those creatures, and amazed by the followings: the tool use that prevents themselves from getting eaten by predators, the coloration that beguiles their natural enemies, and the ink that blocks the sight of diving tourists.

Marine biologists investigating the behavior of octopuses in the Pacific a few years ago have now reached a consensus about the intelligence of those creatures, and amazed by the followings: the tool use that prevented themselves from getting eaten by predators, the coloration that beguiled their natural enemies, and the ink that blocked the sight of diving tourists.

✦中　譯✦ 幾年前，在太平洋調查章魚行為的海洋生物學家們，已經達成了關於那些生物智力的共識，且對於下列事項感到震驚：工具的使用使牠們免於被掠食者吃掉、這包括了蒙蔽牠們天敵的變色和阻擋潛水觀光客視線的墨水。

✦解　析✦ 這個句型中介紹了平行對稱中的時態一致。根據語法要使用過去的時態。在 followings 後，出現表列舉的部分，是由好幾個形容詞子句組成的，而時態需改正成過去式時態才合乎語法。the tool use that prevents themselves from getting eaten by predators, the coloration that beguiles their natural enemies, and the ink that blocks the sight of diving tourists.

✦檢測考點✦ 平行對稱：**時態一致**、時態。

佳句複誦

MP3 039

Marine biologists **investigating** the behavior of octopuses in the Pacific a few years ago **have** now **reached** a consensus about the intelligence of those creatures, and amazed by the followings: the tool use that **prevented** themselves from getting eaten by predators, the coloration that **beguiled** their natural enemies, and the ink that **blocked** the sight of diving tourists.

Unit 40
代名詞指代 ❶：代名詞 it，指代主要子句的主詞

正誤句

KEY 40

Although Best Cellphone's team launched an unprecedented product with much more energy than for any previous movement, they could only sustain this kind of exhausting effort for a few days.

Although Best Cellphone's team launched an unprecedented product with much more energy than for any previous movement, it could only sustain this kind of exhausting effort for a few days.

✦中　　譯✦ 儘管倍斯特手機的團隊發表了史無前例的產品，比起任何先前的活動付出更多的精力，團隊僅能持續這樣令人精疲力竭的努力數天。

✦解　　析✦ 這個句型中介紹了其中一種代名詞指代的用法，這題較難。首句中可以看到 although 引導的副詞子句，主詞為 team，動詞為 launched，than 之後簡潔地加上了 for any previous movement，如果 than 之後要使用主詞+動詞+for any previous movement，動詞要使用過去完成式。錯誤的地方在 for any previous movement, they can only sustain this kind of exhausting effort for a few days.，they 需要改成 **it** 才合乎語法，team 為單數名詞，故要用 it 指代。

✦檢測考點✦ 代名詞指代、簡潔表達。

佳句複誦

Although Best Cellphone's team launched an unprecedented product with much more energy than for any previous movement, it could only sustain this kind of exhausting effort for a few days.

Unit 41
代名詞指代❷：代名詞 it，指代數句後的受詞

正誤句

KEY 41

Rumor has it that it is highly likely that there is a great deal of gold inside ancient tombs and shipwrecks, so treasure hunters all gear up and are planning to get them before extreme weather comes along.

Rumor has it that it is highly likely that there is a great deal of gold inside ancient tombs and shipwrecks, so treasure hunters all gear up and are planning to get it before extreme weather comes along.

✦中　　譯✦ 謠傳在古墓和船的殘骸中非常可能有大量的黃金存在，所以寶藏獵人均作足準備且計畫在極端天氣來臨前取得它。

✦解　　析✦ 這個句型中介紹了其中一項代名詞指代的用法。There is 後使用 a great deal of 修飾 gold，錯誤的地方在 so treasure hunters all gear up and are planning to get them before extreme weather comes along，要將 them 改成 it 才對，them 不可能用於指代 treasure hunters，其指代的對象是 gold。

✦檢測考點✦ 常見慣用語表達、a great deal of 的用法、so 的用法、代名詞指代。

佳句複誦

Rumor has it that it is highly likely that there is a great deal of gold inside ancient tombs and shipwrecks, so treasure hunters all gear up and are planning to get it before extreme weather comes along.

Unit 42
代名詞指代 ❸：代名詞 it 指代的對象離的非常遠且易忽略

正誤句

KEY 42

Financial experts and scholars claim that clay tablets about money found near the pyramid of the ancient Egypt were used to inform people of the importance of stockpiling monthly paychecks and were engraved to prevent people from squandering.

Financial experts and scholars claim that clay tablets about money found near the pyramid of the ancient Egypt were used to inform people of the importance of stockpiling monthly paychecks and were engraved to prevent people from squandering it.

✦中　　譯✦ 財務專家和學者宣稱在古埃及金字塔附近所發現的關於金錢的泥土碑，是用於告知人們儲蓄月薪的重要性以及雕刻在上頭避免人們浪費金錢。

✦解　　析✦ 這題比較難的部分是句子長，而指代的對象又離的非常遠，所以要耐心看完，另外，更有可能被學習者忽略掉要加 it。但是對母語學習者，則較少有這樣情況發生，在 prevent 的句型中，squandering 表示揮霍或浪費，所以是浪費掉了什麼，在句子中指的是浪費掉金錢，而已 it 代替前方提到的 money，要特別小心這題。

✦檢測考點✦ 時態、被動語態、代名詞指代。

佳句複誦

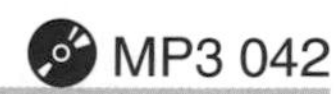

MP3 042

Financial experts and scholars claim that clay tablets about money found near the pyramid of the ancient Egypt were used to inform people of the importance of stockpiling monthly paychecks and were engraved to prevent people from squandering **it**.

Unit 43
代名詞指代④：複數代名詞主格 they

正誤句

KEY 43

Predators, such as lions, still need to watch out for the kicks made by zebras because it can be quite deadly. If the lion gets injured, the wound would prevent it from continuing making a contribution to the pride.

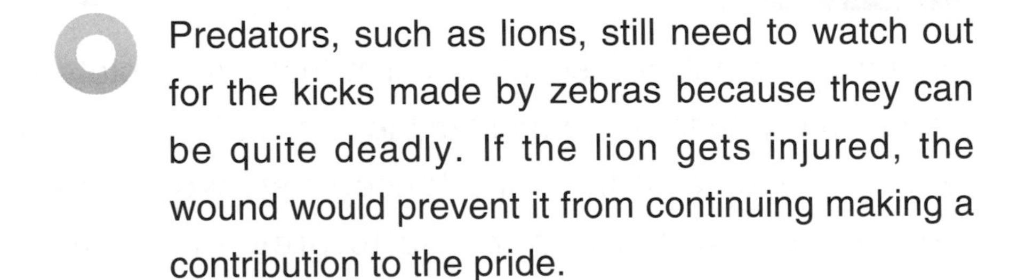

Predators, such as lions, still need to watch out for the kicks made by zebras because they can be quite deadly. If the lion gets injured, the wound would prevent it from continuing making a contribution to the pride.

✦中　　譯✦ 掠食者，例如獅子，仍需要留神由斑馬所發出的踢擊，因為它們可能是相當致命的。如果獅子受到傷害，傷口可能使牠無法在獅群中持續作出貢獻。

✦解　　析✦ 這個句型中介紹了代名詞指代中 they 的用法，其用於指代**複數名詞**且是**主格**。句型中主詞為 predators，其後加上表列舉的部分，主要動詞為 need，錯誤的地方在 Predators, such as lions, still need to watch out for the kicks made by zebras because it can be quite deadly.，it 要改成 they 才合乎語法。後面的 prevent it 中 it 指的是 the lion，這部分的指代無誤。

✦檢測考點✦ 表列舉、代名詞指代、if 的用法、prevent from 的用法。

佳句複誦

Predators, such as lions, still need to watch out for the kicks made by zebras because they can be quite deadly. If the lion gets injured, the wound would prevent it from continuing making a contribution to the pride.

Unit 44
代名詞指代 ❺：複數代名詞受格 them

正誤句

KEY 44

✗ Octopuses are known for their camouflage ability, so sometimes the disguise and coloration can prevent it from getting detected. Dazzling arrays of coloration sometimes paint a vivid picture of the sea world.

○ Octopuses are known for their camouflage ability, so sometimes the disguise and coloration can prevent them from getting detected. Dazzling arrays of coloration sometimes paint a vivid picture of the sea world.

✦中　　譯✦ 章魚以牠們的偽裝能力聞名，所以有時候偽裝和變色能夠使牠們免於被察覺。一系列暈眩奪目的變色有時候替海洋世界描繪了一幅生動的圖畫。

✦解　　析✦ 這題的主詞是 octopuses，動詞是 are，都沒問題，再來要注意的是，接續描述章魚時一定會運用到代名詞來指代章魚，避免一直使用章魚，所以有看到代名詞時一定是複數，如正確句中的 their 和 them，在錯誤句中卻使用了 prevent it，要更正為 them 才是對的。

✦檢測考點✦ 慣用語、代名詞指代、prevent from 的用法。

佳句複誦

MP3 044

Octopuses are known for **their** camouflage ability, so sometimes the disguise and coloration can prevent them from getting detected. Dazzling arrays of coloration sometimes paint a vivid picture of the sea world.

Unit 45
代名詞指代 ❻：複數代名詞所有格 their

正誤句

KEY 45

Dolphins are able to locate fish burying under the sand because its senses are more acute and advanced. To accomplish this involves the use of echolocation, a skill that can be found in other mammals, such as bats.

Dolphins are able to locate fish burying under the sand because their senses are more acute and advanced. To accomplish this involves the use of echolocation, a skill that can be found in other mammals, such as bats.

✦中　　譯✦ 海豚能夠找到埋藏在沙子底下的魚因為牠們的感官更為敏銳和進階。要達到此技能需要回聲定位的使用，一項在其他哺乳類動物中，例如蝙蝠，也能發現到的技能。

✦解　　析✦ 這個句型中介紹了代名詞指代中 their 的用法。句中的主詞為 dolphins，句中的主要動詞為 are，其後 be able to 加原形動詞。Fish 後使用形容詞子句修飾且有省略。錯誤的地方在 Dolphins are able to locate fish burying under the sand because its senses are more acute and advanced.，its 要改成 their 才合乎語法，且根據語意 its 不可能用於指代 fish，指的是 dolphins。

✦檢測考點✦ 慣用語、代名詞指代、不定詞當主詞、同位語的用法、表列舉。

佳句複誦

MP3 045

Dolphins **are able to** locate fish burying under the sand because their senses are more acute and advanced. To accomplish this involves the use of echolocation, a skill that can be found in other mammals, such as bats.

Unit 46
代名詞指代 ⑦：單數名詞的代名詞所有格 its

正誤句

KEY 46

Biodiversity is highly related to the stability of the ecosystem, and their importance can never be underestimated. The more creatures in the ecosystem, the more diverse the ecosystem.

Biodiversity is highly related to the stability of the ecosystem, and its importance can never be underestimated. The more creatures in the ecosystem, the more diverse the ecosystem.

中　　譯　生物多樣性跟生態系統的穩定性是高度相關的，其重要性是不能被低估的。在生態系統中，有著越多樣的生物，生態系統的多樣性越高。

解　　析　這題的主詞是 biodiversity，動詞為單數，也沒錯，在次句中開頭的主詞時，使用了代名詞，而代名詞指的是 biodiversity，所以要使用 its，而在錯誤句中卻使用了 their，是錯誤的，要更正為 their importance。另外要注意的是 the more... the more... 的句型。

檢測考點　慣用語、代名詞指代、the more…the more 句型。

佳句複誦

Biodiversity is highly related to the stability of the ecosystem, and its importance can never be underestimated. The more creatures in the ecosystem, the more diverse the ecosystem.

Unit 47
代名詞指代 ❽：代名詞 it 的其他用法

正誤句

KEY 47

Although hyenas enjoy scavenging leftovers from cheetahs or female lions once in a while, it risks their lives coming closer to four robust male lions, which are still consuming the elephant.

Although hyenas enjoy scavenging leftovers from cheetahs or female lions once in a while, they do not want to risk their lives coming closer to four robust male lions, which are still consuming the elephant.

中　　譯　儘管土狼享受著偶爾從獵豹或雌性獅子那裏獲取的剩餘食物，牠們不想要冒生命的風險去靠近正在攝食大象的四隻強健的雄性獅子。

解　　析　這個句型介紹了「It 無法用於指代前面整個句子」。句子開頭為 although 引導的副詞子句，主詞為 hyenas，動詞為 enjoy，enjoy 後要加動名詞。錯誤的地方在 it risks their lives coming closer to four robust male lions, which are still consuming the elephant，it risks 要改成 they do not want to 才合乎語法。

檢測考點　Although 的用法、代名詞指代、動名詞慣用語、形容詞子句。

佳句複誦

MP3 047

Although hyenas **enjoy** scavenging leftovers from cheetahs or female lions once in a while, they do not want to risk their lives coming closer to four robust male lions, which are still consuming the elephant.

Unit 48
代名詞指代 ❾：ones 用於指代前面出現過的「複數名詞」

正誤句

KEY 48

✗ Desert chameleons cannot always be the one which feed on others because they will encounter their natural enemies, such as rattlesnakes. Desert rattlesnakes normally thrive in extremely dry climates, while their distant cousins, pythons prefer soggier one.

○ Desert chameleons cannot always be the ones which feed on others because they will encounter their natural enemies, such as rattlesnakes. Desert rattlesnakes normally thrive in extremely dry climates, while their distant cousins, pythons prefer soggier ones.

◆中　　譯◆ 沙漠變色龍不可能總是以其他生物為食的生物，因為牠們也會遇到自己本身的天敵，例如響尾蛇。沙漠響尾蛇通常繁盛於極度乾旱的氣候裡，而牠們的遠親，巨蟒偏好潮濕的氣候。

◆解　　析◆ 這個句型中介紹了考生較不熟悉的用法 **ones**，其用於指代「**可數複數名詞**」。錯誤的地方在 Desert chameleons cannot always be the one which feed on others...和 Desert rattlesnakes normally thrive in extremely dry climates, while their distant cousins, pythons prefer soggier one.，兩處的 one 均須改成 ones，第一個 ones 指代 chameleons，第二個 ones 指的是 climates 用於避免重複。

◆檢測考點◆ 代名詞指代、表列舉、while 的用法。

佳句複誦

MP3 048

Desert chameleons cannot always be the ones which feed on others because they will encounter their natural enemies, such as rattlesnakes. Desert rattlesnakes normally **thrive** in extremely dry climates, **while** their distant cousins, pythons prefer soggier ones.

Unit 49
代名詞指代 ⑩：清楚和模糊

正誤句

KEY 49

✕ In this male lion's defense against intruders, he exhibits the swagger and confidence in the first place, and two young male lions are immediately intimidated by the vigor. The situation has demonstrated the importance of confidence in winning.

○ In his defense against intruders, this male lion exhibits the swagger and confidence in the first place, and two young male lions are immediately intimidated by the vigor. The situation has demonstrated the importance of confidence in winning.

✦中　　譯✦ 在防衛入侵者的襲擊時，這隻雄性獅子在一開始就展現出了昂首闊步和自信，而兩隻年輕的雄性獅子立即被這種精力威嚇到。這個情況已經展示了自信對於勝利的重要性。

✦解　　析✦ 這題介紹了代名詞的表達中清楚和模糊，主詞使用清楚的名詞而使用非代名詞是較佳的表達。In **this male lion's defense** against intruders, **he** exhibits the swagger and confidence in the first place，將其修正成 In his defense against intruders, this male lion exhibits the swagger and confidence in the first place 是更好的表達方式。

✦檢測考點✦ 代名詞指代、清楚的表達。

佳句複誦

MP3 049

In **his** defense against intruders, this male lion exhibits the swagger and confidence in the first place, and two young male lions are **immediately intimidated** by the vigor. The situation has demonstrated the importance of confidence in winning.

Unit 50
反身代名詞 ❶：themselves

正誤句

KEY 50

Lion cubs are able to evade multiple dangers by concealing itself under the high grass, whereas lion cubs which is unable to hold their breaths and find safe places to hide will be eaten by other carnivores.

Lion cubs are able to evade multiple dangers by concealing themselves under the high grass, whereas lion cubs which are unable to hold their breaths and find safe places to hide will be eaten by other carnivores.

✦中　　譯✦ 獅子幼獸能夠藉由將自己藏匿在高草原裡來逃避眾多的危險，而無法屏住氣息且找尋安全地方躲藏的獅子幼獸，則會被其他肉食動物吃掉。

✦解　　析✦ 這題的主詞是 cubs，主要動詞是 are，也沒問題，在接續的句子中出現了反身代名詞，此時一定是 themselves 來指代，但是錯誤句中卻使用了 itself。另外要注意的是，whereas 後的主詞 cubs 後使用了形容詞子句，cubs 為複數，所以一定要使用 which are 才對，錯誤句卻使用了 which is，是錯誤的。

✦檢測考點✦ 代名詞指代、whereas 的用法、形容詞子句。

佳句複誦

MP3 050

Lion cubs **are able to** evade multiple dangers by concealing themselves under the high grass, **whereas** lion cubs which are unable to hold their breaths and find safe places to hide will be eaten by other carnivores.

Unit 51
反身代名詞 ❷：itself

正誤句

KEY 51

Unable to defend themselves by the swift wasp's attack, the intelligent tarantula retreats to its lair, resisting to get more stings from the wasp. Tarantulas sometimes even use their fur as weapons to drive away predators or human beings near their dens.

Unable to defend itself by the swift wasp's attack, the intelligent tarantula retreats to its lair, resisting to get more stings from the wasp. Tarantulas sometimes even use their fur as weapons to drive away predators or human beings near their dens.

✦中　　譯✦ 無法防衛對於黃蜂的快速攻擊，機智的狼蛛退回到其巢穴裡頭，抗拒再受到黃蜂更多的螫咬。有時候，狼蛛甚至使用牠們身上的毛當作武器，驅趕靠近牠們洞穴的掠食者或人類。

✦解　　析✦ 這個句型中介紹了反身代名詞 itself 的用法。錯誤的地方在 Unable to defend themselves by the swift wasp's attack, the intelligent tarantula retreats to its lair, resisting to get more stings from the wasp.，themselves 要修正成 **itself** 才合乎語法，因為其指的是主要子句中的 tarantula，是單數，而非複數，如果是使用 tarantulas 則要使用 themselves。

✦檢測考點✦ 慣用語、代名詞指代。

佳句複誦

MP3 051

Unable to defend itself by the swift wasp's attack, the intelligent tarantula retreats to its lair, resisting to get more stings from the wasp. Tarantulas sometimes even use **their** fur as weapons to drive away predators or human beings near their dens.

Unit 52
所有格形式「N+S'」的指代：省略前面已經出現過的名詞

正誤句

KEY 52

✗ Carnivores can sometimes clash with one another, so the fight is not necessarily between carnivores and herbivores. The outcome eventually is neither on the pride of lions' sides nor on the clan of hyena because of a sudden massive rainfall that floods over the area.

○ Carnivores can sometimes clash with one another, so the fight is not necessarily between carnivores and herbivores. The outcome eventually is neither on the pride of lions' sides nor on the clan of hyena's because of a sudden massive rainfall that floods over the area.

✦中　　譯✦ 肉食性動物之間有時彼此衝突，所以戰鬥並不總是發生在肉食性動物和草食性動物。最終的結果不是獅群那頭或是土狼群獲勝，因為突然的豪雨淹沒了該地區。

✦解　　析✦ 這個句型中的主詞為 carnivores，主要動詞為 clash，so 後面的主詞為 fight，動詞為 is。錯誤的地方在 The outcome eventually is neither on the pride of lions' sides nor on the clan of hyena because of a sudden massive rainfall that floods over the area.，hyena 要改成 hyena's/hyena's sides，但是用 hyena's 更佳，且省略掉 sides 的再次使用。

✦檢測考點✦ So 的用法、所有格形式**「N+S'」**的指代、because of。

佳句複誦

Carnivores can sometimes clash with one another, **so** the fight is not necessarily between carnivores and herbivores. The outcome eventually is neither on the pride of lions' sides nor on the clan of hyena's because of a sudden massive rainfall that floods over the area.

Unit 53
同位語 ❶：基礎句型，補充說明

正誤句

KEY 53

✗ Dawson's bees, one of the largest Australian bees, are also known as Dawson's burrowing bees, and it is unique solitary nest-builders, unlike many bees which are gregarious creatures.

○ Dawson's bees, one of the largest Australian bees, are also known as Dawson's burrowing bees, and they are unique solitary nest-builders, unlike many bees which are gregarious creatures.

✦中　　譯✦ 道森蜜蜂，澳洲的最大型蜜蜂，也稱作道森穴居蜜蜂。牠們是獨特的獨居巢穴建造者，與許多群居性的蜜蜂生物不同。

✦解　　析✦ 這個句型中介紹了同位語的用法。首句的主詞為 dawson's bees，同位語為 one of the largest Australian bees，主要動詞為 are。錯誤的地方在 it is unique solitary nest-builders, unlike many bees which are gregarious creatures 要將其改成 they are 才合乎語法，they 指的是 dawson's bees。

✦檢測考點✦ 同位語的用法、慣用語、unlike 的用法。

佳句複誦

Dawson's bees, **one of the largest Australian bees**, are also known as Dawson's burrowing bees, and **they are** unique solitary nest-builders, unlike many bees which are gregarious creatures.

Unit 54
同位語 ❷：擴充句

正誤句

KEY 54

Cannibalization, a phenomenon that occurs among many species, is considered cruel and unkind because it involves consuming species of the same or similar kinds, and Dawson's bees and giant hornets belongs to the category of the cannibalization.

Cannibalization, a phenomenon that occurs among many species, is considered cruel and unkind because it involves consuming species of the same or similar kinds, and Dawson's bees and giant hornets belong to the category of the cannibalization.

✦中　　譯✦ 「同類相殘」是個發生於許多物種的現象，被視為是殘忍且不仁慈的，因為它牽涉到攝食相同或相似的物種，而道森蜜蜂和巨型大黃蜂屬於同類相食的範疇。

✦解　　析✦ 這個句型中也是介紹的同位語的應用句。首句的主詞為 Cannibalization，像這樣的專有名詞通常都會有形容子句/名詞片語形式的同位語來解釋，句子中的主要動詞為 is。錯誤的地方在 Dawson's bees and giant hornets belongs to the category of the cannibalization.。句子中的主詞為 Dawson's bees and giant hornets，所以動詞 belongs 要改成 belong 才合乎語法。

✦檢測考點✦ 同位語的用法、慣用語、代名詞指代。

佳句複誦

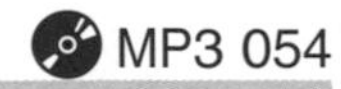

Cannibalization, a phenomenon that occurs among many species, **is** considered cruel and unkind because **it involves** consuming species of the same or similar kinds, and Dawson's bees and giant hornets belong to the category of the cannibalization.

Unit 55
同位語❸：while 句型後加同位語

正誤句

KEY 55

Cannibalization, although considered brutal, is essential in the natural world. While giant hornets stage a series of wars towards honey bees, which is much smaller they are, male Dawson's bees compete with one another to death so that females are able to mate with stronger males.

Cannibalization, although considered brutal, is essential in the natural world. While giant hornets stage a series of wars towards honey bees, which are much smaller than they are, male Dawson's bees compete with one another to death so that females are able to mate with stronger males.

✦中　　譯✦ 同類相殘，儘管被視為是殘忍的，這對於自然界來說是必須的。當巨型大黃蜂對比起自己本身體型遠小的蜜蜂，策劃一系列的戰爭，雄性道森蜜蜂彼此間相互競爭到至死方休，如此一來雌性蜜蜂就能夠與較強壯的雄性交配。

✦解　　析✦ 這個句型中介紹了另一個同位語的應用。首句的主詞為 Cannibalization，中間插入副詞子句，主要子句中主要動詞為 is。錯誤的地方在 While giant hornets stage a series of wars towards honey bees, which is much **smaller** they are，smaller 後要加上 than 才合乎語法，且 which is 要改成 which are 才對，因為 honey bees 為複數名詞。

✦檢測考點✦ Although 的用法、while 的用法和其後加同位語、形容詞子句、比較級。

佳句複誦

Cannibalization, **although** considered brutal, is essential in the natural world. **While** giant hornets stage a series of wars towards honey bees, **which are** much smaller than they are, male Dawson's bees compete with one another to death so that females are able to mate with stronger males.

Unit 56
Like ❶：Like+ 列舉項目，S+V…

正誤句

KEY 56

✕ Like polar bears, brown bears scavenge the corpse of the exceedingly large whale so that it can accumulate enough fat for the winter. Furthermore, both are dormant creatures, so they will go into hibernation before winter and emerge from hibernation when spring arrives.

○ Like polar bears, brown bears scavenge the corpse of the exceedingly large whale so that they can accumulate enough fat for the winter. Furthermore, both are dormant creatures, so they will go into hibernation before winter and emerge from hibernation when spring arrives.

✦中　　譯✦ 像是北極熊，棕熊食腐極大型的鯨魚，這樣一來牠們就能夠在冬天時累積足夠的脂肪。此外，兩者均是冬眠的生物，所以牠們在冬天前會進入冬眠，並且於春天到來時結束冬眠。

✦解　　析✦ 表相似或類比的句型中，常見的就是 like 的使用，但是要注意「比較」的對象，在句型中，polar bears 和 brown bears 就是相對的比較對象，所以是沒問題的，不會造成比較對象的錯誤。使用這個句型也比單純使用「簡單句」更高階。錯誤句中，使用了 it can accumulate 造成的代名詞指代的錯誤，it 無法指代前面的複數名詞 brown bears。

✦檢測考點✦ Like 的用法、so that 的用法、so 的用法、慣用語的用法。

佳句複誦

MP3 056

Like polar bears, brown bears **scavenge** the corpse of the exceedingly large whale **so that** they can accumulate enough fat for the winter. Furthermore, both are dormant creatures, **so** they will have go into hibernation before winter and emerge from hibernation when spring arrives.

Unit 57
Like ❷：加形容詞子句修飾

正誤句

KEY 57

Like pikas, which stockpiles lots of food in the den, ants amass provision for the winter. The discrepancy between the two lies in forces. Pikas are solitary gathers, whereas ants are gregarious creatures, so there is strength in numbers.

Like pikas, which stockpile lots of food in the den, ants amass provision for the winter. The discrepancy between the two lies in forces. Pikas are solitary gathers, whereas ants are gregarious creatures, so there is strength in numbers.

✦中　譯✦ 像是短吻兔，在巢穴中儲藏許多食物，螞蟻為了迎接冬天的到來積聚了糧食。 兩者之間的差異在於力量。短吻兔是單獨的收集者，而螞蟻卻是群居性的生物，所以有著數量的優勢。

✦解　析✦ 除了前個單元的比較對象的用法，這個單元的句型是前個句型的進階用法，在使用 like+N 後，再以一個形容詞子句來修飾該名詞，豐富表達。在句型中可以看見一個形容詞子句修飾 pikas（pikas 和 ants 的比較），還要注意的部分有形容詞子句中動詞的單複數，錯誤句中誤用了 which stockpiles，但 pikas 為複數名詞，所以要改成 which stockpile。

✦檢測考點✦ Like 的用法、形容詞子句、whereas 的用法。

佳句複誦

MP3 057

Like pikas, **which** stockpile lots of food in the den, ants **amass** provision for the winter. The **discrepancy** between the two lies in forces. Pikas are solitary gathers, **whereas** ants are **gregarious** creatures, so there is strength in numbers.

Unit 58
Unlike ❶：unlike+ 列舉項目，S+V…

正誤句

KEY 58

Unlike domesticated elephants, wild elephants have the freedom to do whatever they like on the savanna. Because of its enormous size, wild elephants reign the prairie, and very few animals dare to offend them, including lions.

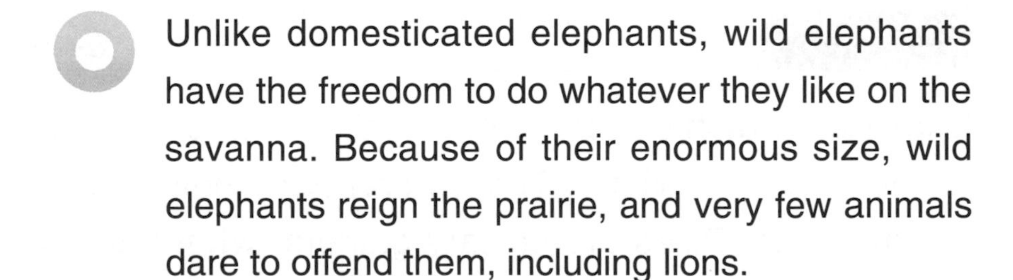

Unlike domesticated elephants, wild elephants have the freedom to do whatever they like on the savanna. Because of their enormous size, wild elephants reign the prairie, and very few animals dare to offend them, including lions.

✦中　　譯✦ 不像家庭馴養的大象，野生大象有著自由，能在大草原上做任何牠們想做的事。因為牠們龐大的體型，野生大象統治著草原，非常少動物膽敢冒犯牠們，包括獅子在內。

✦解　　析✦ 表相異或不同的句型中，常見的就是 unlike 的使用（**用法跟 like 同**），但是要注意「比較」的對象，在句型中是，domesticated elephants 和 wild elephants 兩者間的比較，所以是沒問題的，不會造成比較對象的錯誤。但是在錯誤句中，誤用了 Because of its enormous size 造成了代名詞指涉對象的錯誤，要改成 **their** 才對。

✦檢測考點✦ unlike 的用法、because of 的用法、表列舉。

佳句複誦

MP3 058

Unlike domesticated elephants, wild elephants have the freedom to do whatever they like on the savanna. **Because of their** enormous size, wild elephants reign the prairie, and very few animals dare to offend them, **including** lions.

Unit 59
Unlike ❷：加形容詞子句修飾

正誤句

KEY 59

Unlike desert lizards, which bury themselves under the sand, some forests can run onto the water for several miles to evade predators, such as snakes. Some lizards even have evolved to mimic gestures from other animals to ensure the survival.

Unlike desert lizards, which bury themselves under the sand, some forest lizards can run onto the water for several miles to evade predators, such as snakes. Some lizards even have evolved to mimic gestures from other animals to ensure the survival.

✦中　　譯✦ 不像沙漠的蜥蜴，將其埋在沙子底下，有些森林的蜥蜴能夠在水面上跑幾哩以逃避掠食者，像是蛇。有些蜥蜴甚至已經演化出模仿其他動物的姿勢來確保其生存。

✦解　　析✦ 除了前個單元的比較對象的用法，這個單元的句型是前個句型的進階用法，在使用 **unlike+N** 後，再以一個**形容詞子句**來修飾該名詞，豐富表達。在句型中可以看見一個形容詞子句修飾 desert lizards，子句中的語意也是正確的。主要子句中的名詞就是跟 unlike 後的名詞做比較，錯誤句中使用了 some forests 造成語法上和語意上的錯誤，而且 forests **無法執行後面動詞所表達的動作**。

✦檢測考點✦ unlike 的用法、形容詞子句、表列舉。

佳句複誦

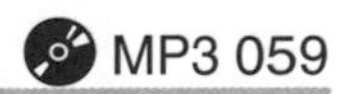

Unlike desert lizards, **which** bury **themselves** under the sand, some forest lizards can run onto the water for several miles to evade predators, such as snakes. Some lizards even have evolved to mimic gestures from other animals to ensure the survival.

Unit 60
Unlike ❸：語序，Unlike+N 的句型中，使用代名詞指代主要子句中的主詞

正誤句

KEY 60

Unlike that in the desert, chameleons in the forest are not that cumbersome and unintelligent, and forests are a fantastic place for it to conceal and camouflage so that almost no predators can detect.

Unlike those in the desert, chameleons in the forest are not that cumbersome and unintelligent, and forests are a fantastic place for them to conceal and camouflage so that almost no predators can detect.

✦中　　譯✦ 不像那些在沙漠的變色龍，森林變色龍沒有那麼笨重且愚蠢。森林對牠們來說是個利於隱藏和偽裝的場所，這樣一來幾乎沒有掠食者能夠察覺。

✦解　　析✦ 這個句型是前幾個句型的延伸（考的是**可比性**，those in the desert 和 chameleons in the forest 須是可比較的），unlike 後使用的不只是名詞，而是以代名詞指代 chameleons，省略的 chameleons 的使用，使更進階的句型表達，且因為是複數名詞，所以要使用 those，錯誤句中誤用成 that，會造成代名詞指代上的錯誤。另一個指代錯誤的地方是 a fantastic place for it to conceal，要更改成 them 才對。

✦檢測考點✦ unlike 的用法、代名詞指代、高階形容詞。

佳句複誦

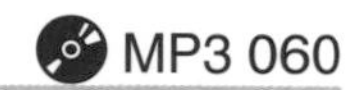

Unlike those in the desert, chameleons in the forest are not that **cumbersome** and **unintelligent**, and forests are a fantastic place for **them** to conceal and camouflage so that almost no predators can detect.

Unit 61
表示相對的片語：In contrast to

正誤句

KEY 61

In contrast to boisterous atmospheres that permeate among a pack of dogs, African lions are motionless and listless, waiting for the sunset. Hunting at a dark night is effortless for the lions, since the vision gives them the advantage.

In contrast to boisterous atmospheres that permeate among a pack of dogs, the vibes among African lions are motionless and listless, waiting for the sunset. Hunting at a dark night is effortless for the lions, since the vision gives them the advantage.

✦中　　譯✦ 喧鬧的氣氛蔓延在一群狗之中，與之相對的是，非洲獅子之間的氣氛是靜止不動且無精打采的，等著太陽下山。在黑暗的夜晚狩獵對於獅子來說是毫不費力的，因為視力給了牠們優勢。

✦解　　析✦ In contrast to 的用法跟 like 和 unlike 同，較少考生使用到，但用於比較相異的兩個物件是很好的表達句，也能避免一直使用 unlike。句型中也是在其後加上名詞後，名詞後再以形容詞子句修飾。錯誤句中誤用了 African lions，此無法跟 boisterous atmospheres that permeate among a pack of dogs 比較。是圍繞在一群狗之間**「的氣氛」**跟非洲獅子之間「的氣氛」做比較。

✦檢測考點✦ In contrast to 的用法、形容詞子句的用法、since 的用法。

佳句複誦

MP3 061

In contrast to **boisterous** atmospheres **that permeate** among a pack of dogs, the vibes among African lions are **motionless** and **listless**, waiting for the sunset. Hunting at a dark night is effortless for the lions, since the vision gives them the advantage.

Unit 62
Contrast 的比較，要注意主詞的單、複數

正誤句

KEY 62

Koalas' laziness and sluggishness contrasts sharply with the nimbleness and agility of the raccoons, two attributes that are related to their washing hands. The diets between them also vary. The former consumes eucalyptus trees, while the latter eats numerous insects, fruits, and fish.

Koalas' laziness and sluggishness contrast sharply with the nimbleness and agility of the raccoons, two attributes that are related to their washing hands. The diets between them also vary. The former consumes eucalyptus trees, while the latter eats numerous insects, fruits, and fish.

✦中　　譯✦ 無尾熊的懶惰和不活潑與浣熊的敏捷和靈活性成了急遽的反差，此兩項特質與其洗手的特性相關。牠們彼此間的飲食也不同。前者攝食尤加利樹葉，而後者食用眾多的昆蟲、水果和魚。

✦解　　析✦ Contrast 是另一個好用的比較用語，蠻直接的表達，因為是當動詞使用，所以要特別注意的是，主詞的單複數，在錯誤句中誤用了 contrasts，但主詞為複數 Koalas' laziness and sluggishness，檢視比較的對象 Koalas' laziness and sluggishness 和 the nimbleness and agility of the raccoons，這點無誤，是兩者間的特質在比較。

✦檢測考點✦ Contrast 的用法、形容詞子句的用法。

佳句複誦

MP3 062

Koalas' laziness and sluggishness contrast sharply with the nimbleness and agility of the raccoons, two attributes that are related to their washing hands. The diets between them also vary. The former consumes eucalyptus trees, while the latter eats numerous insects, fruits, and fish.

Unit 63
表比較相似的片語：Similar to

正誤句

KEY 63

Similar to their long-distance cousins, raccoons are omnivores, and its diets, ranging from huge river crabs to gigantic tarantulas rich in protein. Because of their forelimbs, raccoons are very agile, and they are able to tear a crab apart.

Similar to their long-distance cousins, raccoons are omnivores, and their diets, ranging from huge river crabs to gigantic tarantulas are rich in protein. Because of their forelimbs, raccoons are very agile, and they are able to tear a crab apart.

✦中　　譯✦ 近似於牠們的遠距離親戚，浣熊是雜食性動物，且牠們的飲食，範圍從大型河邊螃蟹到巨型狼蛛。因為牠們的前肢，浣熊非常靈敏，牠們能夠將螃蟹肢解。

✦解　　析✦ 這個句型跟前面提過的類似，只是沒有另一個形容詞子句修飾名詞。錯誤句中誤用了 and **its** diets，造成代名詞指涉的錯誤。回推回去指代的對象是 raccoons，故要改成 their。Diets 後的 ranging from 為形容詞子句的省略，而錯誤句中卻無主要的動詞，故要加上 are 才是正確的表達。

✦檢測考點✦ Similar to 的用法、because of 的用法。

佳句複誦

MP3 063

Similar to their long-distance cousins, raccoons are omnivores, and their diets, ranging from huge river crabs to gigantic tarantulas are rich in protein. **Because of** their forelimbs, raccoons are very agile, and they are able to tear a crab apart.

Unit 64
比較對象 ❶：That

正誤句

KEY 64

✗ The population of crabs is much greater than that of lobsters, so the price of lobsters is bound to be more expensive than crabs. Unless the owner of the seafood restaurant can import lobsters to balance the increasingly expensive prices, he will need to eat up the cost.

○ The population of crabs is much greater than that of lobsters, so the price of lobsters is bound to be more expensive than that of crabs. Unless the owner of the seafood restaurant can import lobsters to balance the increasingly expensive prices, he will need to eat up the cost.

✦中　　譯✦ 螃蟹族群比起龍蝦族群的數量更多，所以龍蝦的價格必定會比螃蟹的價格更昂貴。除非海產店的主人能夠進口龍蝦，以平衡掉日益昂貴的價格，否則他必須要自己承擔下這個成本。

✦解　　析✦ 這題考的是主動詞單複數、代名詞指代和比較級用法。考生常見的是在比較句型中犯了修辭上的錯誤，尤其在 than 後的表達。句型中，第一個句子，主詞為 population，所以比較對象是 The population of crabs 和 The population of lobsters，考生常誤用成 than lobsters，而句中的 that = the population，次句中的 the price of...亦同，後面需使用 than that of crabs，錯誤句中卻僅使用了 crabs，造成修飾錯誤。

✦檢測考點✦ 比較級的用法、代名詞指代。

佳句複誦

MP3 064

The population of crabs **is** much greater than that of lobsters, so **the price** of lobsters is bound to be more expensive than that of crabs. Unless the owner of the seafood restaurant can import lobsters to balance the increasingly expensive prices, he will need to eat up the cost.

Unit 65
比較對象❷：That 加入 before or after 句型的比較

正誤句

KEY 65

✖ Before the rainy season, the life of the carnivores is much worse than herbivores. A lack of food will not do the pride of lions any good because very few lion cubs can survive to the adulthood.

○ Before the rainy season, the life of the carnivores is much worse than that of herbivores. A lack of food will not do the pride of lions any good because very few lion cubs can survive to the adulthood.

✦中　譯✦ 在雨季來臨前，肉食性動物的生活比起草食性動物的生活更糟糕。缺乏食物對於獅群來說沒有任何好處，因為非常少的獅子幼獸能夠活到成年時期。

✦解　析✦ 在有些閱讀文章也會出現更複雜的比較句型，例如像本句型中加入的 before 的表達，將本來的簡單句的比較句型，延伸成了一個副詞子句加上主要子句的句型。主要子句中則包含了**比較句型**。

正常情況下，考生常省略掉 that of 造成不可比較的情況，因為**「肉食動物的生活」**和**「草食性動物」**是無法比較的，應該要改成「草食性動物的生活」才能做比較。錯誤句中僅使用了 herbivores，要修正為 that of herbivores.才對。

✦檢測考點✦ 比較級的用法、代名詞指代。

佳句複誦

MP3 065

Before the rainy season, **the life** of the carnivores **is** much worse than **that of** herbivores. A lack of food will not **do** the pride of lions **any good** because very few lion cubs can survive to the adulthood.

Unit 66
比較對象❸：those 指代前面出現的複數名詞

正誤句

KEY 66

✕ Harmful substances in whales' bodies are immensely greater than that in penguins, according to the law of bioaccumulation. It is well-known that energy loses from one layer of the food chain to the next, while harmful substances accumulate.

○ Harmful substances in whales' bodies are immensely greater than those in penguins', according to the law of bioaccumulation. It is well-known that energy loses from one layer of the food chain to the next, while harmful substances accumulate.

✦中　　譯✦ 鯨魚體內的有害物質比起那些在企鵝體內的有害物質更多，根據生物累積的定律。廣為人知的是，在食物鏈每個層級中，能量逐層流失，而有害物質卻是累積著的。

✦解　　析✦ 這題是一個常見的比較級句型，考的要點是，關於 those 的用法，those 用於替代前方出現過的複數名詞，而這個句型中主要的主詞是 substances，其為複數形式，所以 than 後面要使用 those in...才是正確的，Harmful substances in whales' bodies 和 harmful substances in penguins'兩者間的比較。在錯誤句中，誤用成 that，that 無法替代前面的複數名詞。

錯誤句還有個錯誤是在 penguins，要修正成 penguins' bodies or penguins'，使用 penguins'更簡潔，其省略了 bodies。

✦檢測考點✦ 比較級的用法、代名詞指代。

佳句複誦

Harmful substances in whales' bodies are immensely greater than those in penguins, according to the law of bioaccumulation. It is well-known that energy loses from one layer of the food chain to the next, **while** harmful substances accumulate.

Unit 67
比較對象❹：those 加入 before or after 句型的比較

正誤句

KEY 67

After the migration, food resources in the region are more abundant than that in Africa's National Park. Once again, carnivores will have an adequate amount of food in the following weeks, and it is an endless cycle occurring annually.

After the migration, food resources in the region are more abundant than those in Africa's National Park. Once again, carnivores will have an adequate amount of food in the following weeks, and it is an endless cycle occurring annually.

✦中　　譯✦ 在遷徙之後，這個地區的食物來源比起那些在非洲國家公園的食物來源更為充足。再一次地，接下來的幾週，肉食性動物將會有充足量的食物，而這是每年都會發生的一個無盡的循環。

✦解　　析✦ 在有些閱讀文章也會出現更複雜的比較句型，例如像本句型中加入的 after 的表達，將本來的簡單句的比較句型，延伸成了一個副詞子句加上主要子句的句型。主要子句中則包含了**比較句型**。

這題比較簡單。Those 指代的是前方的複數名詞 **resources**，錯誤句中誤用了 that，that 無法替代前面的複數名詞。

✦檢測考點✦ 比較級的用法、代名詞指代。

佳句複誦

After the migration, food resources in the region are more abundant than those in Africa's National Park. Once again, carnivores will have an **adequate** amount of food in the following weeks, and it is an endless cycle occurring annually.

Unit 68
比較對象❺：更高階的比較 twice ❶

正誤句

KEY 68

✗ The prey is twice as heavy, but one of the experienced female lions have already made a killing bite in such a short time. The abundance of the feast can give this pride of lions a few more days without worrying about food.

○ The prey is twice as heavy, but one of the experienced female lions has already made a killing bite in such a short time. The abundance of the feast can give this pride of lions a few more days without worrying about food.

✦中　　譯✦ 這個獵物是兩倍重，但是其中一隻有經驗的雌性獅子已經在如此短的時間內咬下致命一擊。豐碩的盛宴能讓這個獅群在接下來的幾天都不用擔憂食物的問題。

✦解　　析✦ 這題介紹了考生較少使用到的句型 twice，直接使用 twice as heavy 即是很簡潔且清楚的表達，形容兩倍重。錯誤句中誤用了 one of the experienced female lions **have** already，have 要改成 has，因為 one of...加單數動詞，別被前方的複數名詞干擾到了。

✦檢測考點✦ 比較級的用法（twice）、代名詞指代、one of 的用法。

佳句複誦

MP3 068

The prey is twice as heavy, but **one of** the experienced female lions **has** already made a killing bite in such a short time. The **abundance** of the feast can give this pride of lions a few more days without worrying about food.

Unit 69
比較對象❻：更高階的比較 where+that 子句

正誤句

KEY 69

Keyna's Wildlife Reserves, a place which tourists are capable of witnessing an unprecedented animal migration, is more phenomenal and memorable than that of other Asian Zoos.

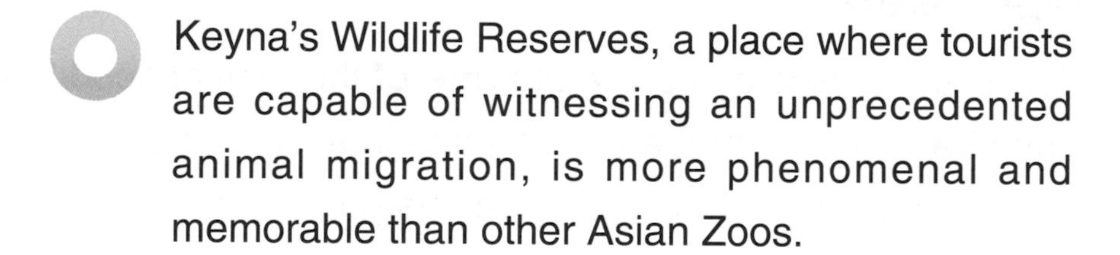

Keyna's Wildlife Reserves, a place where tourists are capable of witnessing an unprecedented animal migration, is more phenomenal and memorable than other Asian Zoos.

✦中　　譯✦ 肯亞的野生生活保護區，一個能夠讓觀光客目睹史無前例的動物遷徙，比起其他動物的野生保護區，更意義非凡且難忘。

✦解　　析✦ 這題在主詞後使用了同位語的表達，主要動詞是 is。錯誤句中的錯誤發生在同位語的句型中 a place 後須改成 **where** 而非 which 才是正確的。另一個錯誤發生在 than that of other Asian Zoos.，此造成了代名詞指代的誤用。Keyna's Wildlife Reserves 和 other Asian Zoos 即是兩個對等的比較對象，野生生活保護區和動物園間的比較，所以要將 that of 刪除才對。

✦檢測考點✦ 比較級的用法、代名詞指代、同位語的用法、主動詞的用法。

佳句複誦

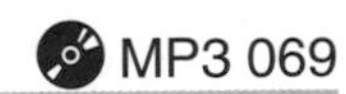
MP3 069

Keyna's Wildlife Reserves, **a place where** tourists are capable of witnessing an unprecedented animal migration, **is** more phenomenal and memorable than other Asian Zoos.

Unit 70 比較對象 ❼：更高階的比較 in addition to+that

正誤句

KEY 70

✗ In addition to geographical factors that influences lions' hunting, there are other factors, such as dry season, rainy season, and intruders. The population of the pride of the lion can fluctuate due to above-mentioned factors, so the graph is important for biologists.

○ In addition to geographical factors that influence lions' hunting, there are other factors, such as dry season, rainy season, and intruders. The population of the pride of the lion can fluctuate due to above-mentioned factors, so the graph is important for biologists.

✦中　譯✦ 除了地理因素影響著獅子的狩獵之外，還有其他因素，例如乾季、雨季和闖入者。獅子的族群會受到上述提及的因素影響而產生波動，所以圖表對於生物學家來說是重要的。

✦解　析✦ In addition to 文法上的用法跟 in contrast to 同，只是兩者的意思不同，in addition to 表的是除了...之外，除了句式更複雜外，也補充說明了主要子句不足的部分。在這個句型中，一樣在句子中使用形容詞子句修辭 in addition to 後的名詞。次句中，也搭配了 due to 的句型。錯誤句中，**geographical factors that influences**，influences 須改成 influence 才合乎語法。

✦檢測考點✦ 比較級的用法（in addition to+that）、代名詞指代、表列舉。

佳句複誦

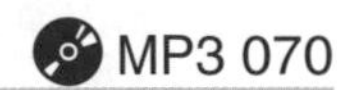

In addition to geographical factors that **influence** lions' hunting, there are other factors, **such as** dry season, rainy season, and intruders. The population of the pride of the lion can fluctuate due to above-mentioned factors, **so** the graph is important for biologists.

Unit 71
比較對象 ❽：更高階的比較
those+ 形容詞子句等複雜修飾

正誤句

KEY 71

✖ Lions in the desert are perseverant and determined than those which inhabit Africa's savannas, a place where water and food resources are usually abundant. When food resources are scarce, sometimes taking down a prey might need quadruple effort.

○ Lions in the desert are more perseverant and determined than those which inhabit Africa's savannas, a place where water and food resources are usually abundant. When food resources are scarce, sometimes taking down a prey might need quadruple effort.

✦中　　譯✦ 比起那些居住在非洲大草原，水和食物來源通常都很充足的獅子來說，沙漠中的獅子更具毅力和決心。當食物來源稀少時，有時候擊倒獵物可能會需要四倍的努力。

✦解　　析✦ 快速看整個句子，句子中有 than 使用了比較級的句型，但是在動詞後，錯誤句 are perseverant and determined 少了 more 修飾兩個形容詞，是錯誤的用法。再來檢視比較的對象 Lions in the desert 和 those which inhabit Africa's savannas 是沒問題的（兩個存活於不同生態體系中的獅子間的比較），其中 those 代替了前方的複數名詞，即 lions。

✦檢測考點✦ 比較級的用法（those+形容詞子句等複雜修飾）、代名詞指代、where 和 when 的用法。

佳句複誦

MP3 071

Lions in the desert are **more** perseverant and determined than those which inhabit Africa's savannas, a place **where** water and food resources are usually abundant. **When** food resources are scarce, sometimes taking down a prey might need quadruple effort.

Unit 72 比較的慣用語：compared with+形容詞子句

正誤句

KEY 72

✗ Compared with cheetahs which are carnivores, lions are gregarious animals and they live in a pride. Lions rarely have to worry about opportunists, such as hyenas, creatures which might steal their food because it is not alone.

○ Compared with cheetahs which are carnivores, lions are gregarious animals and they live in a pride. Lions rarely have to worry about opportunists, such as hyenas, creatures which might steal their food because they are not alone.

✦中　譯✦ 與是肉食性動物的獵豹相比之下，獅子是群居的動物且牠們生活在獅群中。獅子絕少需要擔憂機會主義者，例如土狼，來偷取牠們的食物，因為牠們不是獨自生活。

✦解　析✦ Compared with 是常見的句型，要注意其有 ed 結尾，是慣用語。在句型中，使用了 compared with 搭配名詞，其後以形容詞子句修飾。次句中使用簡單句，搭配了表列舉的項目，其後再以形容詞子句修飾名詞 hyenas。錯誤句中誤用了 because it is not alone，但是 it 無法指代前方複數名詞 lions，要更正為 they are。

✦檢測考點✦ 比較級的用法（compared with）、代名詞指代、形容詞子句、表列舉。

佳句複誦

MP3 072

Compared with cheetahs **which are** carnivores, lions are gregarious animals and they live in a pride. Lions rarely have to worry about opportunists, such as hyenas, creatures **which** might steal their food **because they are** not alone.

Unit 73
比較級的用法 ➊：twice 更精確的使用

正誤句

KEY 73

✖ In the 2009's, the estimation of the price of crabs in Singapore was almost two times greater than the 2010's, but still the crave for the spicy crab dish attracts more people, who neglect increasingly expensive prices.

○ In the 2009's, the estimation of the price of crabs in Singapore was almost twice what it was in the 2010's, but still the crave for the spicy crab dish attracts more people, who neglect increasingly expensive prices.

✦中　譯✦ 在 2009 年間，新加坡螃蟹價格的評估幾乎比起在 2010 年間多了兩倍，但是對於辣螃蟹佳餚的迫切需求吸引了更多人到訪，且無視了日益昂貴的價格。

✦解　析✦ 這題頗難，而且能改寫成好幾種混淆的形式，當中很需要掌握的一點是「比較的對象須一致」和「修飾」。錯誤的地方在 In the 2009's, the estimation of the price of crabs in Singapore was almost two times greater than the 2010's，看似唸起來很順，但是「the estimation of the price of crabs in Singapore」和時間點「the 2010's」兩者是不能進行比較的，須改成正確句中的 twice what it was in 才會是可以比較的。另外要注意的是修飾，有些修飾語會無法修飾 estimation，所以看似唸得很順也不能使用。

✦檢測考點✦ 比較級的用法（twice 更精確的使用）、代名詞指代。

佳句複誦

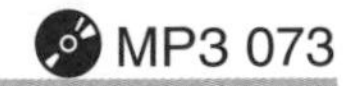

In the 2009's, the estimation of the price of crabs in Singapore was almost twice what it was in the 2010's, but still the crave for the spicy crab dish attracts more people, who neglect increasingly expensive prices.

Unit 74
比較級的用法 ❷ Most of+ 比較級

正誤句

KEY 74

Most of the raccoons in the zoo is more docile and less dexterous than that in the wild; thus, zoologists are planning to capture more wild raccoons and bring them to the establishment so that raccoons can have a diversified appearance in the next performance.

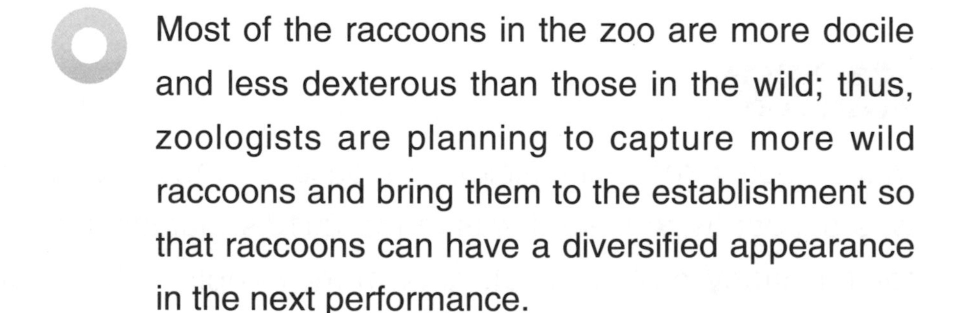

Most of the raccoons in the zoo are more docile and less dexterous than those in the wild; thus, zoologists are planning to capture more wild raccoons and bring them to the establishment so that raccoons can have a diversified appearance in the next performance.

✦中　　譯✦ 在動物園中大多數的浣熊，比起那些在野生的浣熊來說，更溫馴且較不靈敏。因此，動物學家正計畫要捕捉更多的野生浣熊，並將牠們帶至機構裡，這樣一來，浣熊就能夠在下次表演中有更多樣的表現。

✦解　　析✦ 這題是使用比較級的句型且搭配了 most of，而關鍵在於 most of 後所加的名詞片語或名詞才是句中的主詞，句中的主詞並非 most。所以在 Most of the raccoons in the zoo is more docile and less dexterous than that in the wild.中，is 要改正成 are 才合乎語法。另一個需要修正的地方是 that，that 要改成 those，those 指代 the raccoons。（句型中比較的對象為 raccoons in the zoo 和 raccoons in the wild）

✦檢測考點✦ 比較級、most of、代名詞指代。

佳句複誦

MP3 074

Most of the raccoons in the zoo **are** more docile and less dexterous than those in the wild; thus, zoologists are planning to capture more wild raccoons and bring them to the establishment so that raccoons can have a diversified appearance in the next performance.

Unit 75
比較級的用法 ❸：高階副詞加上比較級 immensely greater

正誤句

KEY 75

✗ The number of the blueberries across the river are immensely greater than that of the blueberries in the nearby forest, so squirrels and several animals are trying possible ways to cross the river so that they can hoard enough blueberries before winter.

○ The number of the blueberries across the river is immensely greater than that of the blueberries in the nearby forest, so squirrels and several animals are trying possible ways to cross the river so that they can hoard enough blueberries before winter.

✦中　　譯✦ 跨過河的藍莓數量比起在鄰近樹林的藍莓數量更是多得驚人，所以松鼠和幾種動物正嘗試可能的方式以越河，這樣一來牠們才能在冬天來臨時儲藏足夠的藍莓。

✦解　　析✦ 這題是使用比較級的句型且搭配了 immensely greater，句子中的主詞為 number，所以主要動詞必須使用**單數動詞**，在錯誤句中，卻誤用了 are。接著看代名詞指代的部分，than 後方使用了 that of 沒錯，that 替代了前方的 the number。在後面句子中代名詞指代的部分，so that 後方的 they 指代 squirrels and several animals，所以這點也是沒錯的。

✦檢測考點✦ 比較級的用法（immensely greater）、代名詞指代。

佳句複誦

MP3 075

The number of the blueberries across the river **is immensely greater** than **that of** the blueberries in the nearby forest, so squirrels and several animals are trying possible ways to cross the river so that they can hoard enough blueberries before winter.

Unit 76
比較級的用法 ❹：as...as 的用法 ❶

正誤句

KEY 76

In places as abundant and diverse tropical rainforests, you can easily witness numerous creatures roam in the understory of the forest. The more you explore, the more surprises you are going to get.

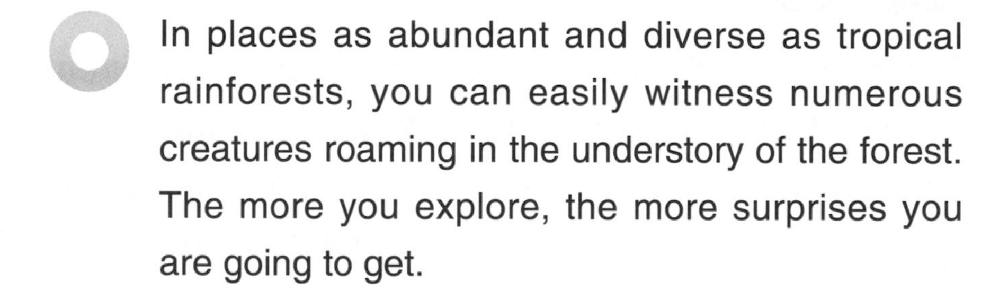

In places as abundant and diverse as tropical rainforests, you can easily witness numerous creatures roaming in the understory of the forest. The more you explore, the more surprises you are going to get.

✦中　　譯✦ 在如同熱帶雨林一樣豐富且多樣的地方，你可以輕易地目睹為數眾多的生物漫遊在樹林的底層。你越是探索，你就越能得到更多的驚喜。

✦解　　析✦ 在這個句型中使用了 as...as，表示兩個列舉的項目是同等的，當中的描述在其中即 as **abundant and diverse** as，在句型中表示兩者均是「豐富且多樣的」，但是在錯誤句中少了第二個 as，須補上。另一個錯誤發生在，主要子句中 numerous creatures roam in the understory of the forest，roam 須改為 roaming，roaming 為 that roam 的省略，是一形容詞子句修飾前方 creatures。

✦檢測考點✦ 比較級的用法（as...as 的用法）、代名詞指代。

佳句複誦

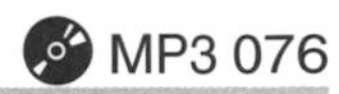
MP3 076

In places as abundant and diverse as tropical rainforests, you can easily witness numerous creatures **roaming** in the understory of the forest. The more you explore, the more surprises you are going to get.

Unit 77
比較級的用法❺：as...as 的用法❷置於主要子句中

正誤句

KEY 77

Mantises are good at capturing small insects, but it can sometimes be as unintelligent as their prey when faced with chameleons. Mantises are unable to responding to the swiftness of the tongue of the chameleon and before they realize it, it is too late.

Mantises are good at capturing small insects, but they can sometimes be as unintelligent as their prey when faced with chameleons. Mantises are unable to respond to the swiftness of the tongue of the chameleon and before they realize it, it is too late.

✦中　　譯✦ 螳螂擅長於捕獲小型昆蟲，但是當牠們在面對變色龍時有時候跟面對牠們的獵物一樣的愚蠢。螳螂無法及時對變色龍舌頭的迅速作出反應，而在牠們意識到時，已經太遲了。

✦解　　析✦ 在這個句型中使用了 as...as，只是改在主要子句中出現，中間的形容詞為 unintelligent，而 when faced with，faced 前方省略了 they are。錯誤句中有兩個錯誤，一個是 but 後使用 it 當主詞，但是 it 無法替代前方出現的複數名詞 mantises，故要改為 they 才對。另一個錯誤是，are unable to 其後要加原形動詞，但是句中卻使用了 V-ing，所以要改為 respond 才對。

✦檢測考點✦ 比較級的用法（as...as 的用法）、代名詞指代。

佳句複誦

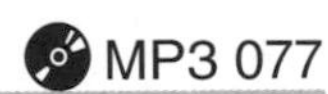

Mantises are good at capturing small insects, but **they** can sometimes be as unintelligent as their prey when faced with chameleons. Mantises are unable to respond to the swiftness of the tongue of the chameleon and before they realize it, it is too late.

Unit 78
比較級的用法 ❻：代名詞指代「複雜」句型

正誤句

KEY 78

✖ Gold coin values in most Asian countries rose almost as fast as, and in some countries even faster than, that outside Asian countries. Therefore, investors are encouraging people to invest in gold this year, telling them it is such a rare opportunity.

◯ Gold coin values in most Asian countries rose almost as fast as, and in some countries even faster than, those outside Asian countries. Therefore, investors are encouraging people to invest in gold this year, telling them it is such a rare opportunity.

✦中　　譯✦ 金幣的價值在大多數的亞洲國家中幾乎以同樣的速度上升，而某些亞洲以外的國家，甚至更為迅速。因此，投資客們正鼓勵人們於今年投資黃金，告訴他們這是如此難得的好機會。

✦解　　析✦ 這個比較句型較複雜，當中包含了 as fast as..和 faster than 考點。首先，先看句子中的主要主詞為 values，動詞使用了過去時態 rose 並搭配成 rose as fast as，表示同樣…快，都沒問題。在錯誤句中，誤用了 **that** outside Asian countries，須改成 those，that 無法代替前面出現過的複數名詞 values。另一個要注意的地方是後面的 them，**them** 代替 **people**。

✦檢測考點✦ 比較級的用法（faster than）、代名詞指代（複雜句型）。

佳句複誦

Gold coin values in most Asian countries rose almost as fast as, and in some countries even faster than, those outside Asian countries. Therefore, investors are encouraging people to invest in gold this year, telling them it is such a rare opportunity.

Unit 79
比較級的用法 ❼：the more...the more...

正誤句

KEY 79

The more you get to know the behavior of the brown bear, the more you will like this creature. Three bear cubs running behind the mother bear are considered adore, and they are just beginning to learn how to catch a salmon in the torrents.

The more you get to know the behavior of the brown bear, the more you will like this creature. Three bear cubs running behind the mother bear are considered adorable, and they are just beginning to learn how to catch a salmon in the torrents.

✦中　　譯✦ 當你更了解棕熊的行為，你就更會去喜歡這樣的生物。跑在熊媽媽後頭的三頭熊寶寶被視為是可愛的，牠們正開始學習如何在激流中抓鮭魚。

✦解　　析✦ 這個句型介紹了考生較少運用到的句型 the more...the more...，建議可以多使用增添句式的表達，要注意句中的平衡的部分。次句的 running 為 which run 的省略，主要動詞為 are，而錯誤句中，誤用了 are considered adore，而 consider 後要加名**形容詞**，故需要修正成 adorable。另外要注意的是，考生常在 consider 後搭配了 as，是錯誤的用法。

✦檢測考點✦ 比較級的用法（the more...the more...）、代名詞指代。

佳句複誦

The more you get to know the behavior of the brown bear, the more you will like this creature. Three bear cubs running behind the mother bear are considered **adorable**, and they are just beginning to learn how to catch a salmon in the torrents.

Unit 80
比較級的用法 8：動名詞當主詞比較級

正誤句

KEY 80

✕ Swimming upstream is incredibly harder than swimming in a motionless lake, so the salmon's way of doing this are worth learning. Salmons are taking the risk of getting washed down and eaten by predators so that they can spawn in the upper river.

〇 Swimming upstream is incredibly harder than swimming in a motionless lake, so the salmon's way of doing this is worth learning. Salmons are taking the risk of getting washed down and eaten by predators so that they can spawn in the upper river.

✦中　　譯✦ 逆游而上比起在靜止的湖泊中更為艱難，所以鮭魚這樣的行為是值得被學習的。鮭魚冒著被沖刷而下和被掠食者捕食的風險，以利牠們在河的上游產卵。

✦解　　析✦ 這個句型介紹了「動名詞當主詞 比較級」的句型，前面提過了動名詞當主詞要用單數動詞，故句中使用 is，這部分沒問題。修飾的部分 incredibly harder 也無誤。再來檢視比較對象 swimming upstream 和 swimming in a motionless lake 兩者間進行比較，也無誤。錯誤句中，在次句誤用了 salmon's way of doing this **are** worth learning，但是句子中的主詞為 way，故要改為單數動詞 is。

✦檢測考點✦ 比較級的用法（動名詞當主詞 比較級）、代名詞指代。

佳句複誦

MP3 080

Swimming upstream **is** incredibly harder than swimming in a motionless lake, so the salmon's way of doing this **is** worth learning. Salmons are taking the risk of getting washed down and eaten by predators so that they can spawn in the upper river.

Unit 81
比較級的用法 ❾：less than 的用法

正誤句

KEY 81

✖ The male lion is getting less than he deserve, but the credit of taking down such a huge elephant should belong to him. Now the pride of lions has plenty of elephant meat to enjoy in the dry season.

○ The male lion is getting less than he deserves, but the credit of taking down such a huge elephant should belong to him. Now the pride of lions has plenty of elephant meat to enjoy in the dry season.

✦中　　譯✦ 雄性獅子並未得到他本該獲得的，但是擊倒如此巨大的大象的功勞應該要歸功於牠。在旱季裡，現在的獅群有許多的大象肉可以享用。

✦解　　析✦ 這個句型也較少考生使用在圖表題中，建議可以多使用。句子中主要主詞為 lion，所以主要動詞要使用 is，這部分沒問題，在錯誤句中，誤用了 **less than he deserve**，有時候唸得很順或寫很順，很容易寫錯，須將其改成 **he deserves**。次句中的主詞為 pride，動詞為 has，這部分沒錯。

✦檢測考點✦ 比較級的用法（less than）、代名詞指代。

佳句複誦

The male lion is getting less than he deserves, but the credit of taking down such a huge elephant should belong to him. Now the pride of lions has plenty of elephant meat to enjoy in the dry season.

Unit 82
比較級的用法 ⑩：more than 的用法

正誤句

KEY 82

✗ Having a fight with crocodiles requires more than just strength and agility, and sometimes lions should not be afraid of water. Cheetahs, on the other hand, is swift and dexterous crocodile catchers.

○ Having a fight with crocodiles requires more than just strength and agility, and sometimes lions should not be afraid of water. Cheetahs, on the other hand, are swift and dexterous crocodile catchers.

✦中　　譯✦ 與鱷魚相鬥不僅僅需要力量和靈活度，有時候獅子必須不怕水。獵豹，另一方面，是個迅速且敏捷的鱷魚捕捉者。

✦解　　析✦ 前面提過了動名詞當主詞要用**單數動詞**，故句中使用 requires，這部分沒問題。句子中使用了 more than 表示不僅僅是…，次句中使用了與之相對的片語 on the other hand，表示獵豹和獅子的相襯，但在錯誤句中，主要動詞誤用成 **is**，但是句中的主要主詞為複數名詞 **cheetahs**，所以要使用複數動詞 are。

✦檢測考點✦ 比較級的用法（more than）、代名詞指代。

佳句複誦

Having a fight with crocodiles requires more than just strength and agility, and sometimes lions should not be afraid of water. Cheetahs, on the other hand, **are** swift and dexterous crocodile catchers.

Unit 83
比較的承轉詞：whereas 等的用法

正誤句

KEY 83

Hornets are known for their ability to cannibalize other bee colonies, whereas lions are not noted for eating creatures similar to their own, such as cheetahs and leopards. Lions might kill cheetahs when they threatened, but they will not eat them.

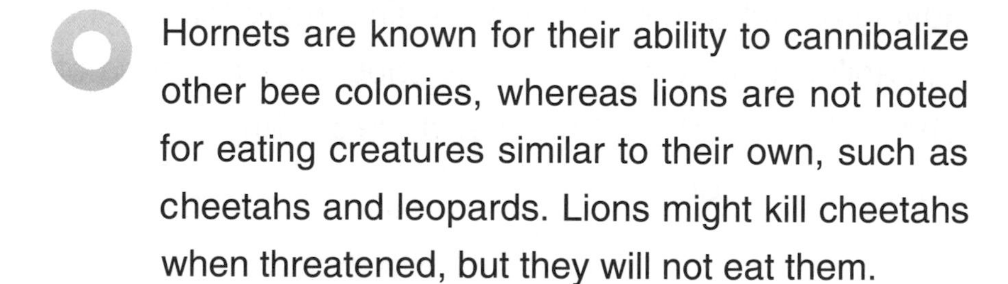

Hornets are known for their ability to cannibalize other bee colonies, whereas lions are not noted for eating creatures similar to their own, such as cheetahs and leopards. Lions might kill cheetahs when threatened, but they will not eat them.

✦中　　譯✦ 大黃蜂以牠們同類相食其他蜜蜂群落的能力而廣為人知，而獅子卻不以牠們攝食類似於牠們的物種，例如獵豹和美洲豹聞名。獅子可能會在受到威脅時殺死獵豹，但是卻不會食用牠們。

✦解　　析✦ 這個句型介紹了 whereas 表示兩個不同物種間的比較。主要句子中的主詞為 hornets，動詞使用 are，這部分沒問題。Whereas 子句中，主詞為 lions，句中動詞為 are 這部分也是正確的，其後加了 similar to...和表列舉的項目。錯誤句中，誤用了 Lions might kill cheetahs **when** they **threatened**，看似正確(S+V)，但其實應該要寫成 they are/feel **threatened**，其中 they are/feel 可以省略，要小心這點。

✦檢測考點✦ 比較級的用法（搭承轉詞）、代名詞指代。

佳句複誦

Hornets are known for their ability to cannibalize other bee colonies, whereas **lions** are not noted for eating creatures similar to their own, **such as** cheetahs and leopards. Lions might kill cheetahs when threatened, but they will not eat the them.

Unit 84
表示列舉的句型 ❶：for example

正誤句

KEY 84

✗ In the forest, for example, we are warned not to disturb the colony of hornets or mother bears with newborn cubs, fearing that can engender a serious consequence. Visiting the forest without causing any harm are considered the best.

○ In the forest, for example, we are warned not to disturb the colony of hornets or mother bears with newborn cubs, fearing that can engender a serious consequence. Visiting the forest without causing any harm is considered the best.

✦中　　譯✦ 例如，在森林裡，我們被警告不要擾動大黃蜂群或是攜帶著剛出生幼熊的母熊，唯恐此舉會產生嚴重的後果。參觀森林卻不引起任何傷害被視為是最棒的。

✦解　　析✦ 這個句型介紹了表列舉（for example）、表否定的不定詞（not to+V）、動名詞當主詞。前面句子語法均正確。錯誤句中 Visiting the forest without causing any harm are considered the best.誤用了複數動詞，須將其改為單數動詞 is。

✦檢測考點✦ 表列舉（for example）、不定詞（not to+V）、動名詞當主詞。

佳句複誦

In the forest, for example, we are warned **not to disturb** the colony of hornets or mother bears with newborn cubs, fearing that can **engender** a serious consequence. **Visiting** the forest without causing any harm **is** considered the best.

Unit 85
表示列舉的句型 ❷：such as

正誤句

KEY 85

In Africa, we are amazed by how giraffes defending itself against predators, such as a pride of lions and hyenas. Giraffes can lash out and give deadly kicks that break the bone of the leg of the predator.

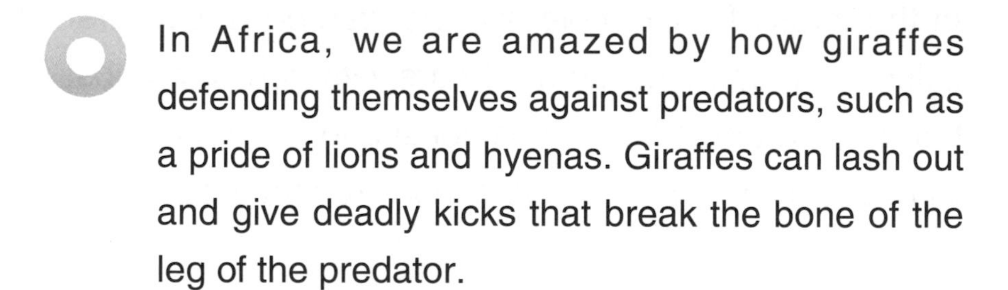

In Africa, we are amazed by how giraffes defending themselves against predators, such as a pride of lions and hyenas. Giraffes can lash out and give deadly kicks that break the bone of the leg of the predator.

✦中　　譯✦ 在非洲，我們對於長頸鹿面對像獅子和土狼這類的掠食者時，如何防衛自己感到驚奇。長頸鹿可能猛擊且給予致命踢擊，讓掠食者腳上的骨頭碎裂。

✦解　　析✦ 這個句型介紹了表列舉的（such as），首句中要注意反身代名詞要使用 themselves，因為 giraffes 為複數。在錯誤句中誤用了 itself，是錯誤的用法。另外需要注意的部分是在 give deadly kicks that break，break 需要用複數，因為 kicks 為複數名詞。

✦檢測考點✦ 表列舉（such as）、慣用語。

佳句複誦

In Africa, we are **amazed** by how giraffes defending **themselves** against predators, such as a pride of lions and hyenas. Giraffes can **lash out** and give deadly kicks that break the bone of the leg of the predator.

Unit 86
表示列舉的句型 ❸：including

正誤句

KEY 86

In Africa, lions are powerful rulers, dominating places where water and food resources are plentiful, but it sometimes has to avoid the confrontation with other creatures, including elephants and rhinos.

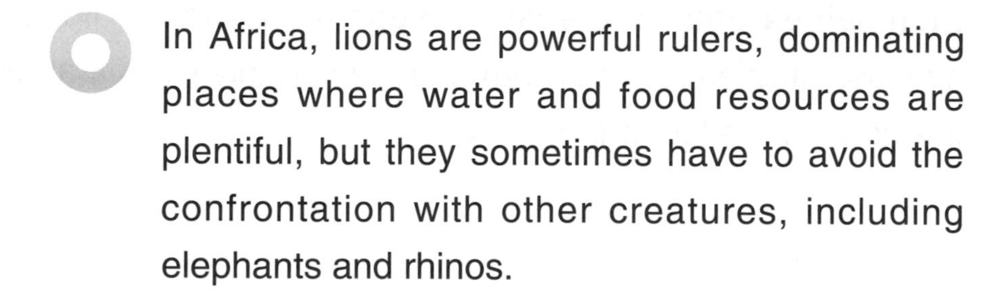

In Africa, lions are powerful rulers, dominating places where water and food resources are plentiful, but they sometimes have to avoid the confrontation with other creatures, including elephants and rhinos.

✦中　　譯✦ 在非洲，獅子是強而有力的統治者，佔據著水源和食物來源充足的地區，但是牠們有時候必須要避開其他生物，包含大象和犀牛。

✦解　　析✦ 這個句型介紹了表列舉的（**including**），錯誤的部份發生在 but it sometimes has to avoid the confrontation with，但是 it 無法指代前方的複數名詞，所以要改為複數的 they 才能指代 lions，改成複數後，後面的動詞也要更正為 have。

✦檢測考點✦ 表列舉（including）、where 和 but 的用法。

佳句複誦

MP3 086

In Africa, lions are powerful rulers, **dominating** places **where** water and food resources are plentiful, **but they** sometimes have to avoid the confrontation with other creatures, including elephants and rhinos.

Unit 87
表示列舉的句型 ❹：like

正誤句

KEY 87

Tarantulas, like scorpions, are equipped with powerful venom, a natural design that makes them invincible in some circumstances, but wasps can repeated sting them without getting harm by their venomous fangs.

Tarantulas, like scorpions, are equipped with powerful venom, a natural design that makes them invincible in some circumstances, but wasps can repeatedly sting them without getting harmed by their venomous fangs.

✦中　　譯✦ 狼蛛，像毒蠍一樣，配有著強大的毒素，天然的設計讓牠們在有些情況下是無可匹敵的，但是黃蜂能夠重複地螫牠們在其毒牙攻擊下仍毫髮無傷。

✦解　　析✦ 這個句型介紹了表列舉的（**like**），只是先表達名詞，like 置於句中，主要主詞為 Tarantulas，故動詞要使用複數 are，這部分也沒問題。錯誤句的誤用發生在 can repeated sting them without getting harm by their venomous fangs，句中的主要動詞為 sting，故要用副詞修飾該動詞，所以要改成 repeatedly 才對，另外是 getting harm 要改成 harmed，即過去分詞的形式才合乎語法。

✦檢測考點✦ 表列舉（**like**）、慣用語、同位語、but 的用法、代名詞指代。

佳句複誦

MP3 087

Tarantulas, like scorpions, **are equipped with** powerful venom, a natural design that makes them invincible in some circumstances, **but** wasps can **repeatedly** sting **them** without getting **harmed** by their venomous fangs.

Unit 88
強調的用法：especially

正誤句

KEY 88

In India, mother sloth bears are powerful fighters, especially when it is with their newborn babies. Normally, baby bears stay on the back of the mother bear and receive such an extensive care.

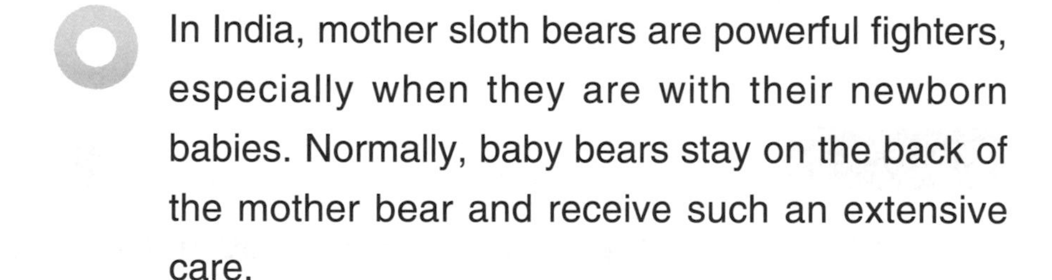

In India, mother sloth bears are powerful fighters, especially when they are with their newborn babies. Normally, baby bears stay on the back of the mother bear and receive such an extensive care.

✦中　　譯✦ 在印度，母懶熊是強而有力的鬥士，尤其是當牠們與剛出生的幼熊一起時。通常，幼熊待在母熊的背上且受到如此完善的照顧。

✦解　　析✦ 這個句型介紹了**強調**的用法：especially，通常會搭 when。主要句子中的主詞為 bears，故動詞使用 are，這部分無誤。錯誤句的誤用發生在 when it is with，而 it 無法指代前方的複數名詞 bears，所以是錯誤的，要更正為 **they are**。

✦檢測考點✦ 強調的用法：especially。

佳句複誦

MP3 088

In India, mother sloth bears are powerful fighters, especially when **they are** with their newborn babies. Normally, baby bears stay on the back of the mother bear and receive such an extensive care.

Unit 89
句型拓展 ❶：使用承轉詞 however

正誤句

KEY 89

The attack from behind; however, does not gives the male tiger an upper hand, and in an instant, he is surprisingly bitten by the mother sloth bear. The male tiger manages to avoid a further bite and makes a threatening roar.

The attack from behind; however, does not give the male tiger an upper hand, and in an instant, he is surprisingly bitten by the mother sloth bear. The male tiger manages to avoid a further bite and makes a threatening roar.

✦中　　譯✦ 然而，從後面的攻擊，無法讓雄性老虎占上風，而驚人的是，牠瞬間已經被母懶熊咬到了。雄性老虎設法要閃避下一波的咬勢，且發出威脅性的咆嘯。

✦解　　析✦ 這個句型介紹了 however 表示語氣的轉折，且置於句中，而錯誤句的誤用發生在 does not gives the male tiger an upper hand，does 為助動詞其後要加原形動詞，所以要更正為 give。另一個要注意的是，出題要點可以更改為 no matter how，而在表示無論如何的意思時 however=no matter how，但是如果是表示然而的意思時，however 不等於 no matter how。

✦檢測考點✦ 承轉詞 however、被動語態、慣用語。

佳句複誦

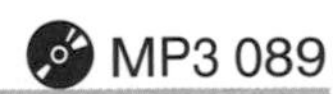

The attack from behind; however, does not **give** the male tiger **an upper hand**, and in an instant, he **is surprisingly bitten** by the mother sloth bear. The male tiger manages to avoid a further bite and makes a **threatening** roar.

Unit 90
句型拓展 ❷：使用 on the other hand

正誤句

KEY 90

Nimbleness and swiftness, on the other hand, are male impala pursue because these two attributes are related to mating and survival. Slow runners are susceptible to an attack made by predators.

Nimbleness and swiftness, on the other hand, are what male impala pursue because these two attributes are related to mating and survival. Slow runners are susceptible to an attack made by predators.

✦中　　譯✦ 敏捷和速度，另一方面，是雄性黑斑玲追求的，因為這兩項特質關係到了交配和生存。慢速的跑者易於受到掠食者所發出的攻擊。

✦解　　析✦ 這個句型介紹了 on the other hand 的用法，且置於句中，而錯誤句的誤用發生在 are male impala purse because，句子中出現了雙動詞 are 和 pursue 夾雜主詞的句型，故要修正成使用名詞子句將其改成 are what male impala purse 才是正確且合乎語法的使用。次句的主要主詞為 runners，動詞為 are，這部分語法是正確的。

✦檢測考點✦ On the other hand 的用法、because 的用法。

佳句複誦

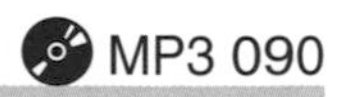
MP3 090

Nimbleness and swiftness, **on the other hand**, are **what** male impala pursue because these two attributes are related to mating and survival. Slow runners **are** susceptible to an attack made by predators.

Unit 91
句型拓展 ❸：使用 although

正誤句

KEY 91

Although newborn bears receive such an extensive care by their mother, they eventually have to stand on their own feet, probably around two years old. Tigers still pose a threat to it because sloth bears at this stage are still not that strong.

Although newborn bears receive such an extensive care by their mother, they eventually have to stand on their own feet, probably around two years old. Tigers still pose a threat to them because sloth bears at this stage are still not that strong.

✦中　　譯✦ 儘管剛出生的熊有著牠們母親的完善照顧，牠們最終還是必須要要自食其力，可能大約是在兩歲左右的時候。在這個時期，懶熊還沒那麼強壯，所以老虎對於牠們來說仍是威脅。

✦解　　析✦ 這個句型介紹了 although，為一連接詞引導副詞子句，搭配一主要子句。在錯誤句中，第二個句子中誤用了 Tigers still pose a threat to it because sloth bears at this stage，根據句意和語法，造成威脅的對象是 bears，it 無法指代 bears，所以要改成 them（受格）才是正確的。

✦檢測考點✦ Although 的用法、because 的用法。

佳句複誦

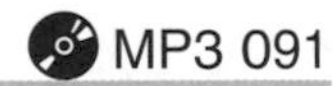

Although newborn bears receive such an extensive care by their mother, they eventually have to stand on their own feet, probably around two years old. Tigers still pose a threat to **them** because sloth bears at this stage are still not that strong.

Unit 92
句型拓展 ❹：使用 but

正誤句

KEY 92

Lions are good at hunting prey on open savanna and prairie, but are unskillful in the water. Striding into the water makes most of the lions discomfort and normally they do not want to get their fur drenched.

Lions are good at hunting prey on open savanna and prairie, but are unskillful in the water. Striding into the water makes most of the lions uncomfortable and normally they do not want to get their fur drenched.

✦中　　譯✦ 獅子擅長於在開放式的無樹平原和大草原上狩獵，但是卻不擅於在水中狩獵。 大步涉向水裡讓大多數的獅子感到不舒服，通常牠們不想要毛被沾的濕透。

✦解　　析✦ 這個句型介紹了 but，首句的主詞 lions 搭配動詞 are...。次句中以動名詞當主詞，故使用單數動詞 makes，到這邊為止都沒問題。錯誤句中誤用了 Striding into the water makes most of the lions discomfort，discomfort 是名詞，但是根據語法在 make 和其受詞後所接的詞性必須要是形容詞才對，所以要將其改成 uncomfortable。

✦檢測考點✦ but 的用法、動名詞當主詞的用法。

佳句複誦

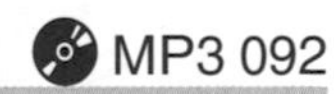

Lions **are good at** hunting prey on open savanna and prairie, but are **unskillful** in the water. Striding into the water makes most of the lions uncomfortable and normally they do not want to get their fur drenched.

Unit 93
句型拓展 ❺：使用 when

正誤句

KEY 93

When a pride of lions initiates an attack, there is a force of cooperation that can intimidate inexperienced herbivores. Confusion make the kill a lot easier because prey will flee in disarray.

When a pride of lions initiates an attack, there is a force of cooperation that can intimidate inexperienced herbivores. Confusion makes the kill a lot easier because prey will flee in disarray.

✦中　　譯✦ 當一個獅群發動攻擊，有股合作的力量能夠威嚇到不具經驗的草食性動物。慌亂讓獵殺更為容易，因為獵物會亂竄。

✦解　　析✦ 這個句型介紹了 when，為一連接詞引導副詞子句，搭配一主要子句。在首句中主詞和動詞的使用均正確。但在錯誤句中，將第二個句子的動詞誤用成複數動詞 make，但是主詞是單數名詞 confusion，所以要改成 makes 才是正確的。

✦檢測考點✦ when 的用法、there is 的用法、慣用語。

佳句複誦

MP3 093

When a pride of lions **initiates an attack**, there is **a force of cooperation** that can intimidate inexperienced herbivores. Confusion **makes** the kill a lot easier because prey will **flee in disarray**.

Unit 94
句型拓展 ❻：使用 whether

正誤句

KEY 94

✗ Whether desert lions are able to tackle down the large giraffe in sight, the attack has demonstrated its desperation for food. Chasing the giraffe in the desert might be accompanied with swirls of dust which impair the eyesight of the lions.

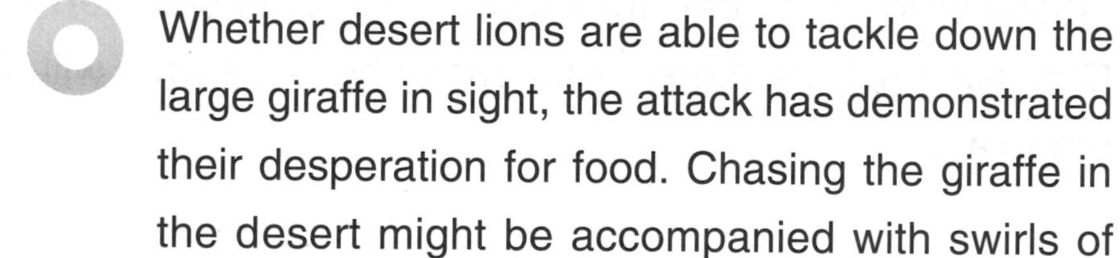

○ Whether desert lions are able to tackle down the large giraffe in sight, the attack has demonstrated their desperation for food. Chasing the giraffe in the desert might be accompanied with swirls of dust which impair the eyesight of the lions.

✦中　　譯✦ 不論沙漠獅子是否能夠對付視線所及的大型長頸鹿，此攻擊都已經展現出了牠們對於食物的迫切度。在沙漠中追逐長頸鹿可能伴隨而來的是盤旋而起的沙塵，阻礙了獅子的視線。

✦解　　析✦ 這個句型介紹了 whether 的用法，子句中的主詞為 lions 其後加上複數動詞 are，在主要子句中主詞為 attack，搭配單數動詞 has。在錯誤句中，誤用了 has demonstrated its desperation for food，根據語意指代的對象不可能是 giraffe 而是 lions，故要將其改成 their 才是正確的。

✦檢測考點✦ whether 的用法、代名詞指代、形容詞子句。

佳句複誦

Whether desert lions are able to tackle down the large giraffe in sight, the attack has demonstrated **their** desperation for food. Chasing the giraffe in the desert might be accompanied with swirls of dust which impair the eyesight of the lions

Unit 95
句型拓展 ❼：使用 who

正誤句

KEY 95

Potential candidates who can immediately boost the morale and bring the instant profit to the company are what investors crave for. Candidates wanting to be the future CEO consider this as a rare opportunity.

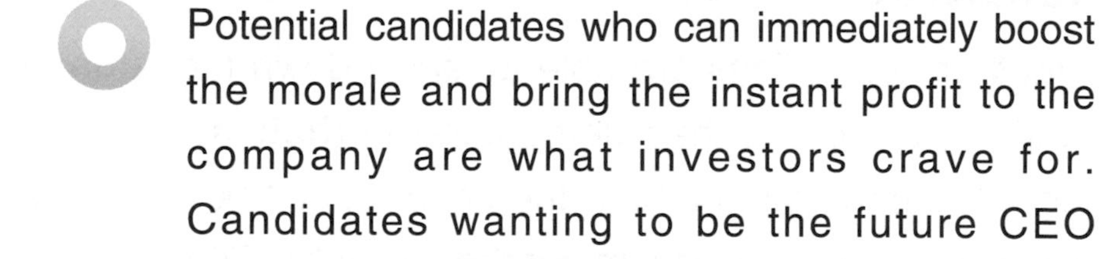

Potential candidates who can immediately boost the morale and bring the instant profit to the company are what investors crave for. Candidates wanting to be the future CEO consider this a rare opportunity.

✦中　　譯✦ 能夠即刻提升士氣和替公司帶來立即利潤的潛在候選人是投資客們所渴望的。想要當 CEO 的都將此視為是罕見的機會。

✦解　　析✦ 這個句型介紹了 who 的用法，candidates 為人，所以其後關係代名詞要使用 who。句子中的主要動詞為 are，這部分也無誤。次句中的主詞也是 candidates，動詞為複數 consider。錯誤句中誤用了，consider this as a rare opportunity.，根據語法使用要將 as 刪除，考生很容易跟類似 think of...as 等用法混淆，而加上了 as。

✦檢測考點✦ 形容詞子句 who、形容詞子句的省略。

佳句複誦

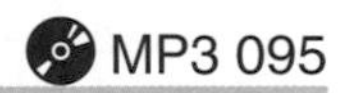
MP3 095

Potential candidates who can immediately **boost the morale** and bring the instant profit to the company are what investors crave for. Candidates wanting to be the future CEO consider this a rare opportunity.

Unit 96
句型拓展 ❽：使用 since

正誤句

KEY 96

Since lions cannot outrun cheetahs under most circumstances, they prefer to choose prey that is easily captured. Wildebeests and buffalos are favored by lions, since it is not dexterous and can be taken down by a combined force.

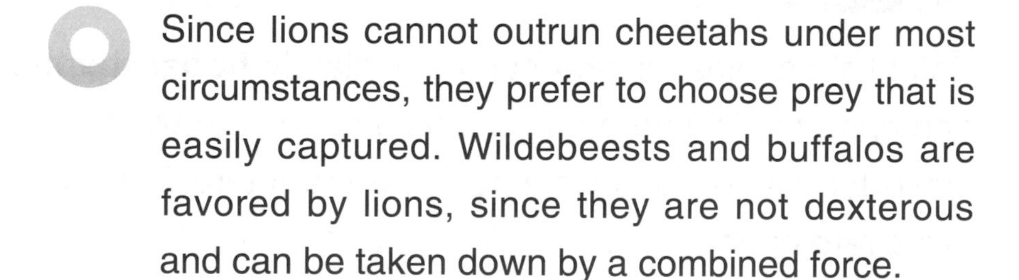

Since lions cannot outrun cheetahs under most circumstances, they prefer to choose prey that is easily captured. Wildebeests and buffalos are favored by lions, since they are not dexterous and can be taken down by a combined force.

✦中　　譯✦ 在大多數情況下，既然獅子無法跑過獵豹，牠們情願選擇較易捕獲的獵物。獅子較偏好牛羚和水牛，因為牠們比較沒那麼敏捷且能被結合的力量擊倒。

✦解　　析✦ 這個句型介紹了 since 的用法，since 在句中表示既然，主要子句中主詞以 they 代替前面出現的複數名詞 lions。錯誤句中誤用了 since it is not dexterous and can be taken down by a combined force，但是 since 子句中的主詞指的是前方的 **wildebeests and buffalos**，所以要改成 they are 才是正確的。

✦檢測考點✦ 副詞子句 since、形容詞子句、被動語態。

佳句複誦

Since lions cannot outrun cheetahs under most circumstances, they prefer to choose prey that is easily captured. Wildebeests and buffalos **are favored by** lions, since **they are** not dexterous and can be taken down by a combined force.

Unit 97
句型拓展 ❾：使用 so that

正誤句

KEY 97

King snakes are packaged with complex protein so that they are not afraid of getting bitten by other venomous snakes. The swallowing of a rattlesnake by a king snake are somewhat unbearable and cruel.

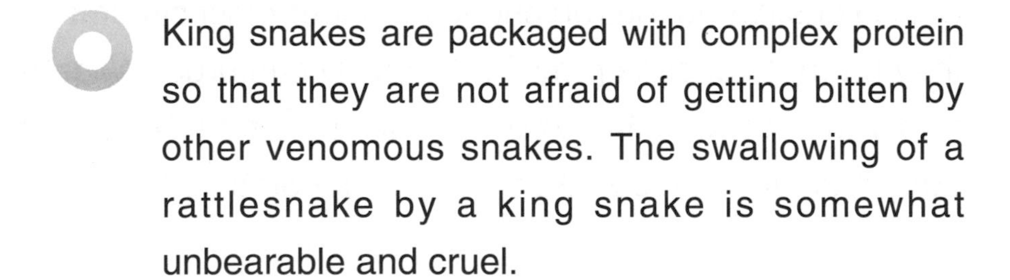

King snakes are packaged with complex protein so that they are not afraid of getting bitten by other venomous snakes. The swallowing of a rattlesnake by a king snake is somewhat unbearable and cruel.

✦中　　譯✦ 王蛇包裹著複合蛋白質，這樣一來牠們就不需要懼怕被其他有毒的毒蛇咬到。王蛇吞食響尾蛇有點讓人覺得難以忍受且殘酷。

✦解　　析✦ 這個句型介紹了 so that 的用法，首句的主詞為 King snakes，so that 後須使用複數的代名詞 they，這部分也無誤。錯誤句中誤用了 The swallowing of a rattlesnake by a king snake are somewhat unbearable and cruel，但是根據語法要使用單數動詞 is，因為主詞是 swallowing。

✦檢測考點✦ So that 的用法、慣用語。

佳句複誦

MP3 097

King snakes **are packaged with** complex protein so that they are not afraid of getting bitten by other venomous snakes. The swallowing of a rattlesnake by a king snake is somewhat unbearable and cruel.

Unit 98
句型拓展 ⑩：使用 because of

正誤句

KEY 98

Because of the winning experience, the disciple is able to outshine other contestants in both extreme weather conditions and on high cliffs. Familiarity with the geography give him an upper hand, avoiding one stab after another.

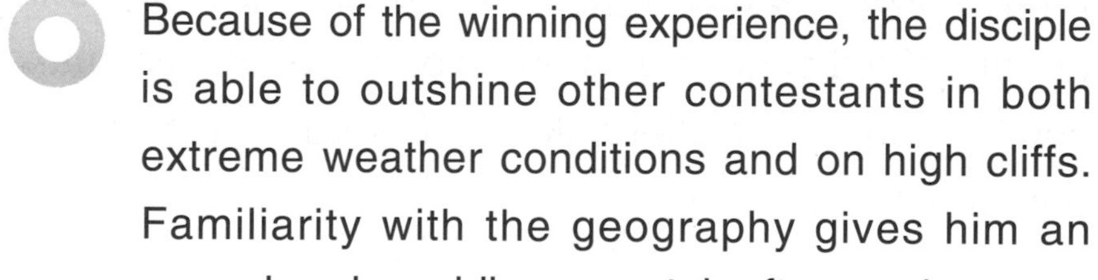

Because of the winning experience, the disciple is able to outshine other contestants in both extreme weather conditions and on high cliffs. Familiarity with the geography gives him an upper hand, avoiding one stab after another.

◆中　　譯◆ 因為贏過的經驗，這位門徒能夠在極端天候狀況和高峭壁處都表現得比其他競賽者優秀。熟悉地勢讓他佔上風，避開了接連的突刺。

◆解　　析◆ 這個句型介紹了 because of 的用法，其後要加上名詞片語或名詞，要小心別跟 because 用法混淆了，because 後加的是子句，所以包含了 S+V。主要子句的主詞為 disciple，故使用單數動詞 is，be able to 後加上原形動詞，這部分也無誤。在次句中，誤用了 Familiarity with the geography give him an upper hand，因為主詞是 familarity 所以要使用單數動詞 gives 才是正確的。

◆檢測考點◆ Because of 的用法、慣用語的用法。

佳句複誦

MP3 098

Because of the winning experience, the disciple is able to outshine other contestants in both extreme weather conditions and on high cliffs. Familiarity with the geography **gives** him **an upper hand**, avoiding one stab after another.

Unit 99
複雜句型❶：By+ving

正誤句

KEY 99

✖ By analyze how two swordsmen react to the attack, the disciple eventually comes up with something more advanced, astounding several masters on the spot. Leaping the ground can offer them a few seconds to react, but two unintelligent swordsmen is not intelligent enough to think about it at the moment.

○ By analyzing how two swordsmen react to the attack, the disciple eventually comes up with something more advanced, astounding several masters on the spot. Leaping the ground can offer them a few seconds to react, but two unintelligent swordsmen are not intelligent enough to think about it at the moment.

✦中　譯✦ 藉由分析兩位劍士如何應對攻擊，這個門徒最終想出了一些更為進階之法，震驚了在現場的幾位大師。從地面躍起能提供他們幾秒的反應時間，但是兩位愚蠢的劍士在當下沒有聰明到能想到此舉。

✦解　析✦ 這個句型介紹了 **by+ving** 的用法，一開始就可以看到錯誤，by analyze 須改成 **analyzing** 才是正確的。另外，還有一個地方出現錯誤，but two unintelligent swordsmen is not intelligent enough to think about it at the moment.，swordsmen 是**複數名詞**，所以其後要使用複數的動詞，故須將其改成 are 才合乎語法。

✦檢測考點✦ By+ving 的用法、比較級。

佳句複誦

By analyzing how two swordsmen react to the attack, the disciple eventually comes up with something **more advanced**, astounding several masters on the spot. Leaping the ground can offer them a few seconds to react, but two **unintelligent** swordsmen **are** not intelligent enough to think about it at the moment.

Unit 100
複雜句型❷：For those

正誤句

KEY 100

✕ For those who is less capable, it is advisable that they stay closer to the main building so that they will not get harmed by concealed weapons and poisonous arrows discharged by the enemies.

○ For those who are less capable, it is advisable that they stay closer to the main building so that they will not get harmed by concealed weapons and poisonous arrows discharged by the enemies.

✦中　　譯✦ 對於那些能力較不出色者，建議他們待在較靠近主要大樓的地方，這樣一來他們就能免於敵人所發出的暗器或是毒箭。

✦解　　析✦ 這個句型介紹了 for those 的用法，錯誤的發生在 For those who is less capable，those 代表指代的是複數名詞，故 who 後面須使用**複數的動詞**才是正確的，所以要將其改成 are 才合乎語法。而在後面的句子中 concealed weapons and poisonous arrows discharged by the enemies.，arrows 後省略了 which are。

✦檢測考點✦ for those、比較級、命令句、so that、關係代名詞省略。

佳句複誦

For those who **are** less capable, it is **advisable** that they stay closer to the main building **so that** they will not get harmed by concealed weapons and poisonous arrows **discharged** by the enemies.

Unit 101
複雜句型 ❸：just like

正誤句

KEY 101

The male desert chameleon stealthy walks into labyrinth-like shrubs, but he is just like prey falling onto the meticulously-crafted trap set by the zebra snake which awaits him there.

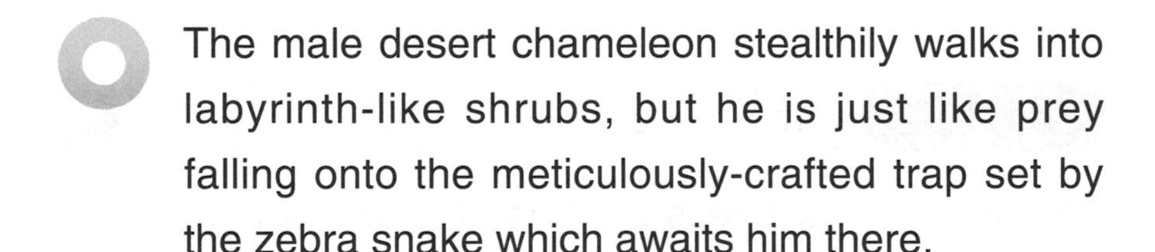

The male desert chameleon stealthily walks into labyrinth-like shrubs, but he is just like prey falling onto the meticulously-crafted trap set by the zebra snake which awaits him there.

✦中　　譯✦ 雄性的沙漠變色龍偷偷摸摸地走入迷宮般的灌木叢中，但是牠就像是掉入由在那裏等待著牠的斑馬蛇所精心編織的陷阱裏頭的獵物。

✦解　　析✦ 這個句型介紹了 just like，錯誤的地方在 The male desert chameleon stealthy walks into labyrinth-like shrubs，而根據語法要使用副詞修飾動詞才是正確的用法，故要將其改成 stealthily walks。

另外，後面形容詞子句省略的部分在 set by 前面，省略了 which is。而 zebra snake 為單數，所以關係代名詞子句中的動詞要用單數 awaits。

✦檢測考點✦ 關係代名詞省略、just like。

佳句複誦

MP3 101

The male desert chameleon **stealthily** walks into labyrinth-like shrubs, but he is just like prey falling onto the **meticulously-crafted** trap set by the zebra snake which **awaits** him there.

Unit 102
複雜句型❹：if

正誤句

KEY 102

✗ If the kingdom of the male lion is overthrown, considerable lion cubs whether male or female, will be executed by new rulers, intruders of physically stronger male lions. Sometimes geography can be a great barrier that separate the clash between the pride of the lions and the male wanderers.

○ If the kingdom of the male lion is overthrown, considerable lion cubs whether male or female, will be executed by new rulers, intruders of physically stronger male lions. Sometimes geography can be a great barrier that separates the clash between the pride of the lions and the male wanderers.

✦中　　譯✦ 如果雄性獅子的王國被推翻了，大量的獅子幼獸，不論是雄性或雌性，都將被新的統治者，體魄更為強壯的雄性獅子闖入者，處決而亡。有時候地勢可以區隔獅群和雄性流浪者之間的衝突。

✦解　　析✦ 這個句型介紹了 If，首句的主詞為 kingdom，其後的動詞要用被動語態 is overthrown，次句的主詞為 cubs，中間又有 whether，主要動詞為 will be，句子後方又以同位語修飾 rulers。錯誤的發生在，geography can be a great barrier that separate the clash，因為 barrier 是單數，故 separate 要改成單數動詞 separates 才是正確的。

✦檢測考點✦ If 的用法、whether 的用法、形容詞子句。

佳句複誦

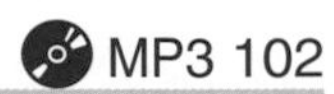
MP3 102

If the kingdom of the male lion is overthrown, considerable lion cubs **whether** male or female, will **be executed by** new rulers, intruders of physically stronger male lions. Sometimes geography can be a great barrier **that separates** the clash between the pride of the lions and the male wanderers.

Unit 103
複雜句型❺：名詞子句當主詞

正誤句

KEY 103

What honeybees lack in physique and strength are well-known, but the number and defending strategies make up for their weaknesses. Increasing honeybees that enhance the temperature around a giant hornet can be quite lethal, since its body can endure a sudden surge of heat.

What honeybees lack in physique and strength is well-known, but the number and defending strategies make up for their weaknesses. Increasing honeybees that enhance the temperature around a giant hornet can be quite lethal, since its body can endure a sudden surge of heat.

✦中　譯✦ 蜜蜂所欠缺的體格和力量是廣為人知的，但是數量和防護的策略補足了牠們的缺點。大黃蜂周遭的溫度因日益增多的蜜蜂而提高了，這可以是相當致命的，因為大黃蜂的身體無法承受突然激增的熱度。

✦解　析✦ 這個句型介紹了名詞子句當主詞，而名詞子句當主詞要加上單數動詞，錯誤句中誤用了 What honeybees lack in physique and strength are well-known，根據語法要將 are 改回 is，要注意別被前面的兩個名詞 physique and strength 所干擾到了。

✦檢測考點✦ 名詞子句當主詞、慣用語、形容詞子句、since 的用法。

佳句複誦

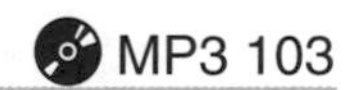
MP3 103

What honeybees lack in physique and strength is well-known, but the number and defending strategies **make up for** their weaknesses. Increasing honeybees **that enhance** the temperature around a giant hornet can be quite lethal, **since** its body can endure a sudden surge of heat.

Unit 104
複雜句型 ❻：使用 with

正誤句

KEY 104

With the increase number of buffalos running down the valley, it is hard for a pride of lions to insulate the buffalo and make a kill. Fortunately, there are still some buffalos which is far lagged behind, so lions can still have a chance.

With the increasing number of buffalos running down the valley, it is hard for a pride of lions to insulate the buffalo and make a kill. Fortunately, there are still some buffalos which are far lagged behind, so lions can still have a chance.

✦中　　譯✦ 隨著日益增加的水牛奔跑在山谷中，對於獅群來說很難隔離出一頭水牛且獵殺之。幸運的是，仍有些水牛遠遠落後，所以獅子仍有機會。

✦解　　析✦ 這個句型介紹了 with 的用法，錯誤的地方在 With the increase number of buffalos running down the valley，根據語法 increase 須改成 increasing，increasing 表日益增多的，當作形容詞修飾 number。另一個錯誤的地方發生在 there are still some buffalos which **is** far lagged behind，根據語法 is 要改成 are，因為 buffalos 為複數名詞。

✦檢測考點✦ With 的用法、比較級原級的用法、形容詞子句。

佳句複誦

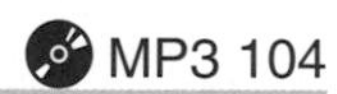

With the **increasing** number of buffalos running down the valley, it is hard for a pride of lions to insulate the buffalo and make a kill. Fortunately, there are still some buffalos which are **far** lagged behind, so lions can still have a chance.

Unit 105
複雜句型 ❼：使用 in addition to

正誤句

KEY 105

In addition to the impending danger that poses a threat to the survival of the desert rat, heat in the desert can do a colossal damage in such a short time. Some rats shade itself under the bush or wait until the sunset.

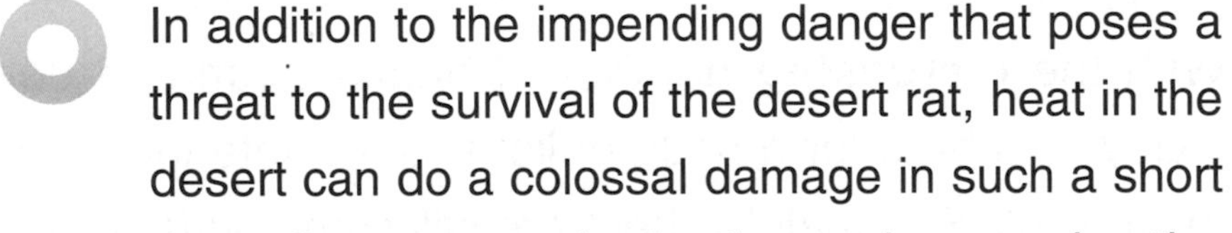

In addition to the impending danger that poses a threat to the survival of the desert rat, heat in the desert can do a colossal damage in such a short time. Some rats shade themselves under the bush or wait until the sunset.

✦中　　譯✦ 除了迫近的危險對於沙漠鼠的生存所造成的威脅，沙漠中的熱度在短時間內能造成大幅度的損害。有些老鼠以灌木庇陰或是等到太陽下山。

✦解　　析✦ 這個句型介紹了 in addition to 的用法，也是搭配了形容詞子句作修飾，子句中 danger 為單數，故後面的修飾是 that poses，主要子句的主詞為 heat。錯誤的地方在 Some rats shade itself under the bush or wait until the sunset，itself 無法替代 rats，因為 rats 為複數名詞，故要將其改為 **themselves** 才是正確的。

✦檢測考點✦ in addition to 的用法、慣用語、代名詞指代。

佳句複誦

In addition to **the impending danger** that poses a threat to the survival of the desert rat, heat in the desert can **do a colossal damage** in such a short time. Some rats **shade** themselves under the bush or wait until the sunset.

Unit 106
複雜句型❽：使用 in addition

正誤句

KEY 106

✖ In addition, ghastly pythons are formidable in that they can initiate an attack in an instant, making prey breathless. Crocodiles near the river all want to avoid the confrontation when it see a giant python comes closer.

○ In addition, ghastly pythons are formidable in that they can initiate an attack in an instant, making prey breathless. Crocodiles near the river all want to avoid the confrontation when they see a giant python comes closer.

✦中　　譯✦ 此外，恐怖的巨蟒是令人畏懼的，因為牠們能夠一下子就發動攻擊讓獵物無法呼吸。靠近河的鱷魚在看到一條大型巨蟒更靠近時，都想要避開正面衝突。

✦解　　析✦ 這個句型介紹了 in addition 的用法，別跟前個單元的句型混淆了。In addition 表示此外，在句子中當作承轉詞。句中的主詞為 pythons，動詞為 are，句中使用了 in that，其意思同 because，副詞子句中的主詞以 they 代替 pythons。次句中的主詞為 crocodiles，主要動詞為 want，錯誤的地方在 when it see a giant python comes closer.，要將 it 改為 they 才合乎語法。

✦檢測考點✦ in addition 的用法、慣用語、代名詞指代。

佳句複誦

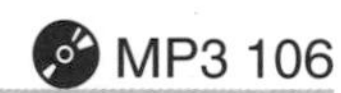
MP3 106

In addition, ghastly pythons are formidable in that they can **initiate an attack** in an instant, making prey breathless. Crocodiles near the river all want to avoid the confrontation when **they** see a giant python comes closer.

Unit 107
複雜句型 ❾：使用 otherwise

正誤句

KEY 107

Crocodiles dominating the swamp have to be careful about the presence of giant pythons; otherwise, they could be the meals for those killers. Surprisingly, one of the giant pythons zeros in on the crocodile and twist it in the next second.

Crocodiles dominating the swamp have to be careful about the presence of giant pythons; otherwise, they could be the meals for those killers. Surprisingly, one of the giant pythons zeros in on the crocodile and twists it in the next second.

✦中　　譯✦ 鱷魚佔據著沼澤必須要對於巨蟒的出現相當小心翼翼，否則牠們可能會成了那些殺手的餐點。令人吃驚的是，其中一條大型巨蟒將注意力集中在鱷魚身上，下秒中纏繞住那頭鱷魚。

✦解　　析✦ 這個句型介紹了 otherwise 的用法，句子中的主詞為 crocodiles 為複數，後面加上了形容詞子句修飾主詞，主要動詞為 have。次句中主詞為 they，根據語意 they 指的是 pythons。錯誤的地方在 one of the giant pythons zeros in on the crocodile and twist it in the next second.，根據語法 twist 要改成 twists。

✦檢測考點✦ otherwise 的用法、慣用語、代名詞指代。

佳句複誦

Crocodiles dominating the swamp have to be careful about the presence of giant pythons; otherwise, they could be the meals for those killers. Surprisingly, one of the giant pythons zeros in on the crocodile and **twists it** in the next second.

Unit 108
複雜句型 ⑩：使用 so

正誤句

KEY 108

✗ Lions cannot maintain a steady velocity in the chase for the prey, so they have to come up with a different strategy. Cheetah, on the other hand, are able to run after the prey in a fast, constant speed.

○ Lions cannot maintain a steady velocity in the chase for the prey, so they have to come up with a different strategy. Cheetahs, on the other hand, are able to run after the prey in a fast, constant speed.

✦中　　譯✦ 獅子無法在追逐獵物期間維持持續穩定的速度，所以牠們必須要想出另一則對策。獵豹，另一方面，能夠以快速且穩定的速度追逐獵物。

✦解　　析✦ 這個句型介紹了 so 的用法，句子中的主詞為 Lions 為複數，so 後面的句子主詞為 they，they 代替前方的複數名詞 lions。次句使用了 on the other hand，錯誤的地方在句子中的主詞，Cheetah, on the other hand, are able to run after the prey in a fast, constant speed，因為句中的主要動詞為 are，所以主詞要改為複數名詞 cheetahs 才對。

✦檢測考點✦ 慣用語、so 的用法、on the other hand 的用法。

佳句複誦

MP3 108

Lions cannot **maintain a steady velocity** in the chase for the prey, **so** they have to come up with a different strategy. Cheetahs, **on the other hand**, **are** able to run after the prey in a fast, constant speed.

Unit 109
複雜句型 ⓫：使用 because

正誤句

KEY 109

✗ This place is picturesque and attractive, and the cleanliness of the lake and the serenity of the valley makes people lingered. Swans swimming on the lake make this place even more beautiful. Fresh mollusks in the lake provide great sources of food for those swans because of they are on the list of their favorite food.

○ This place is picturesque and attractive, and the cleanliness of the lake and the serenity of the valley make people lingered. Swans swimming on the lake make this place even more beautiful. Fresh mollusks in the lake provide great sources of food for those swans because they are on the list of swans' favorite food.

✦中　　譯✦ 這個地方是風景如畫且引人入勝的，而湖泊的乾淨度和山谷的寧靜讓人們流連忘返。游在湖面上的天鵝讓這個地方更為美麗。在湖泊裡，新鮮的軟體動物對於那些天鵝來說是很棒的食物來源，因為那是牠們食物清單上最喜好的食物。

✦解　　析✦ 這個句型介紹了 because 的用法搭配複雜句型，要區隔 because 和 because of 的差異，錯誤的地方在 Fresh mollusks in the lake are a great source of food for those swans because of they are on the list of their favorite food.，because of 須改成 because，因為句子中為一子句，而 because of 後面加名詞或名詞片語。

✦檢測考點✦ Because、高階名詞、形容詞子句。

佳句複誦

This place is picturesque and attractive, and the cleanliness of the lake and the serenity of the valley make people **lingered**. Swans swimming on the lake make this place even more beautiful. Fresh mollusks in the lake provide great sources of food for those swans **because** they are on the list of swans' favorite food.

Unit 110
慣用語❶：less likely 比較級

正誤句

KEY 110

The fragrance of these kinds of flowers is less likely to lure certain insects than flowers found near the huge spider den. Insects are grotesquely attracted by the aroma and eventually get killed by the huge spider.

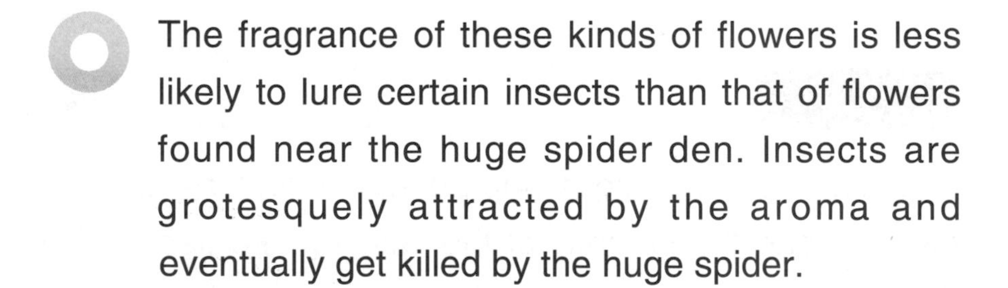

The fragrance of these kinds of flowers is less likely to lure certain insects than that of flowers found near the huge spider den. Insects are grotesquely attracted by the aroma and eventually get killed by the huge spider.

✦中　　譯✦ 這些種類花朵的芳香比起在巨型蜘蛛巢穴中所發現的花朵較不可能引誘特定的昆蟲。昆蟲奇特地受到那樣的氣味吸引，而最終被巨型蜘蛛殺死。

✦解　　析✦ 這個句型介紹了 less likely 的用法，主要的主詞為 fragrance，句中的動詞要用單數動詞 is，要注意的是 than 後面，錯誤句中的 than flowers found near the huge spider den.要修正成 than that of flowers found near the huge spider den.才是正確的，不然會造成修飾上的錯誤，是兩種花的花香氣在作比較。

✦檢測考點✦ 主動詞一致、代名詞指代、比較級。

佳句複誦

The fragrance of these kinds of flowers is less likely to lure certain insects than **that of** flowers found near the huge spider den. Insects are grotesquely attracted by the aroma and eventually get killed by the huge spider.

Unit 111
慣用語 ❷：be used as「用於⋯」

正誤句

KEY 111

✗ Some poisons can be used as antidotes, so there is another saying that everything has good sides and bad sides. Using some poisons to dilute the effects of certain poisons can sometimes be deemed as a plausible solution.

○ Some poisons can be used as antidotes, so there is another saying that everything has its good sides and bad sides. Using some poisons to dilute the effects of certain poisons can sometimes be deemed as a plausible solution.

✦中　　譯✦ 有些毒藥能當作是解毒劑，所以有一個種說法是，每件事物都有其好的和壞的一面。使用有些毒藥去淡化有些特定毒藥的效果，有時候可能被視為是可行的解決辦法。

✦解　　析✦ 這個句型介紹了 be used as 的用法，as 後要加名詞，錯誤的地方在 everything has good sides and bad sides.，everything 後少了 its，its 是代替 everything，也要避免誤用成 their。另外要注意的是，be deemed as 這時候要加上 as 才是正確的，但如果使用 consider 則要刪除 as 才是正確的用法。

✦檢測考點✦ 慣用語、there be 句型。

佳句複誦

Some poisons can be used as antidotes, so there is another saying that everything has **its** good sides and bad sides. Using some poisons to dilute the effects of certain poisons can sometimes be deemed as a plausible solution.

Unit 112
慣用語❸：be widely known「更廣為人知」

正誤句

KEY 112

The master is more widely known than the one who rarely makes his presence known, but fame does not equal as capability. After several rounds of the bare-handed fight, the famous master cannot seem endure the attack and manages to use a venomous concealed weapon.

The master is more widely known than the one who rarely makes his presence known, but fame does not equal as capability. After several rounds of the bare-handed fight, the famous master cannot seem to endure the attack and manages to use a venomous concealed weapon.

✦中　　譯✦ 這位大師比起那位較鮮少露面的大師更廣為人知，但是名聲不等同於能力。在幾個回合的赤手空拳的搏鬥後，名師幾乎無法抵擋攻勢，而設法使用有毒的暗器。

✦解　　析✦ 這個句型介紹了 be widely known，主詞為 the master 其後加上單數動詞 is，than 後以 the one 表達，跟 master 互為比較對象。子句中動詞為 makes 也合乎語法。錯誤的地方在於 the famous master cannot seem endure the attack，seem 要改成 seem to 才合乎語法，而未加 to 也會造成句中有雙動詞的現象。

✦檢測考點✦ 比較級、慣用語、after 的用法。

佳句複誦

MP3 112

The master is more widely known than the one who rarely makes his presence known, but fame does not equal as capability. **After** several rounds of the bare-handed fight, the famous master cannot **seem to** endure the attack and manages to use a venomous concealed weapon.

Unit 113
慣用語❹：apart from「除了⋯之外」

正誤句

KEY 113

Apart from learning martial arts skills from his own sect, John Wang kept many people in the dark and studied advanced sword movements he found behind the huge waterfall. For swordsmen, a rare encounter was essential and pivotal.

Apart from learning martial arts skills from his own sect, John Wang kept many people in the dark and studied advanced sword movements he had found behind the huge waterfall. For swordsmen, a rare encounter was essential and pivotal.

✦中　　譯✦ 除了學習他自己派別的武功之外，約翰・王將許多人蒙騙在鼓裡，並且研習了他在巨大瀑布後方發現的高階的劍術招式。對劍士們來說，奇遇是必須且關鍵的。

✦解　　析✦ 這個句型中介紹了 apart from，apart from 後面加名詞或 ving，主要子句中的主詞為 Wang，動詞為 kept 和 studied。錯誤的地方在 studied advanced sword movements he found behind the huge waterfall.，found 改成 had found 會更好，因為是表示他早先發現的…，所以要使用過去完成式，過去完成式所發生的時間早於過去式，所以是先發現瀑布後的高明劍招，之後才研習招式。

✦檢測考點✦ 慣用語（apart from）、慣用語（keep...in the dark）、時態。

佳句複誦

Apart from learning martial arts skills from his own sect, John Wang **kept** many people **in the dark** and **studied** advanced sword movements he had **found** behind the huge waterfall. For swordsmen, a rare encounter was essential and pivotal.

Unit 114
慣用語❺：when it comes to「當 ... 提到」

正誤句

KEY 114

✖ When it comes to kingsnakes, it often reminds people of its phenomenal attack to rattlesnakes. Kingsnakes do not have venom, but nature gifts them with uncanny chemical substances that makes them immune from the bite of other venomous snakes.

○ When it comes to kingsnakes, it often reminds people of their phenomenal attack to rattlesnakes. Kingsnakes do not have venom, but nature gifts them with uncanny chemical substances that make them immune from the bite of other venomous snakes.

✦中　　譯✦ 當提到王蛇時，通常會讓人們想到牠們攻擊響尾蛇時的非凡之擊。王蛇並沒有毒，但是自然界賦予牠們神奇的化學物質，讓牠們免疫於其他毒舌的噬咬。

✦解　　析✦ 這個句型中介紹了 when it comes to 其後加上了名詞或 ving，錯誤的地方在 it often reminds people of its phenomenal attack，要將 its 改成 their 才符合語法，因為 kingsnakes 是複數名詞。另一個錯誤是 uncanny chemical substances that makes them immune from，makes 要改成 make 才符合語法。

✦檢測考點✦ 慣用語（when it comes to）、慣用語（remind… of）、but 的用法、代名詞指代、形容詞子句。

佳句複誦

MP3 114

When it comes to kingsnakes, it often **reminds** people **of** **their** phenomenal attack to rattlesnakes. Kingsnakes do not have venom, **but** nature gifts them with **uncanny** chemical substances that make them immune from the bite of other venomous snakes.

Unit 115
慣用語❻：be used for「用於…」

正誤句

KEY 115

The treasure map is used for conceal something important in the cave, beguiling people into believing that there is actually an abundance of wealth in another place. Also, authentic treasures are guarded by two giant dragons, which is difficult to tackle.

The treasure map is used for concealing something important in the cave, beguiling people into believing that there is actually an abundance of wealth in another place. Also, authentic treasures are guarded by two giant dragons, which are difficult to tackle.

✦中　　譯✦ 藏寶圖是用於隱匿洞穴中一些重要的東西，蒙蔽人們，讓其相信在另一個地方確實有著豐碩的財富。而且，真正的寶藏是由兩頭難對付的巨龍看守著。

✦解　　析✦ 這個句型中介紹了 be used for，錯誤的地方在 The treasure map is used for conceal something，conceal 要改正成 concealing，因為 for 為介係詞，其後要加名詞或 ving 才合乎語法。另一個錯誤的地方在 are guarded by two giant dragons, which is difficult to tackle，is 要改正成 are 才合乎語法，因為前面的 dragons 為複數名詞。

✦檢測考點✦ 慣用語（be used for）、慣用語（beguile…into）、被動語態、形容詞子句。

佳句複誦

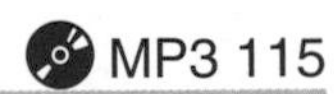
MP3 115

The treasure map is used for concealing something important in the cave, **beguiling** people **into** believing that there is actually an abundance of wealth in another place. Also, authentic treasures **are guarded by** two giant dragons, which **are** difficult to tackle.

Unit 116
慣用語 ❼：contrary to「與 ... 相對」

正誤句

KEY 116

✖ Contrary to what people might think, the treasure map is actually a bogus one, leading numerous treasure hunters to entirely wrong directions. They actually believe that after taking down four sacred monsters, real treasures is within an arm length.

○ Contrary to what people might think, the treasure map is actually a bogus one, leading numerous treasure hunters to entirely wrong directions. They actually believe that after taking down four sacred monsters, real treasures are within an arm's length.

✦中　　譯✦ 與人們可能的想法相左，寶藏圖實際上是贗造的，將為數眾多的寶藏獵人引導到全然錯誤的方向。寶藏獵人實際上相信，在擊倒四聖獸後，真正的寶藏就近在咫尺了。

✦解　　析✦ 這個句型中介紹了 contrary to，主要子句的主詞為 map，其後使用單數動詞 is。次句的 they 指的是 treasure hunters。錯誤的地方在 real treasures is within an arm length.，動詞要改成 are 才合乎語法，因為 treasures 為複數名詞。另外要修正的地方是慣用語 arm 要改成 arm's 才是正確的。

✦檢測考點✦ 慣用語（contrary to）、慣用語（within an arm's length）。

佳句複誦

MP3 116

Contrary to what people might think, the treasure map is actually a bogus one, leading numerous treasure hunters to entirely wrong directions. They actually believe that after taking down four sacred monsters, real treasures **are** within an arm's length.

Unit 117
慣用語❽：due to the fact that+子句

正誤句

KEY 117

✗ Due to he is in such a lower stance, the elegance and craftiness of the movement does not work its trick, making the character capable than the amateur swordsman. After making a huge leap and regrouping the strength, the character chops off the right arm of the amateur.

○ Due to the fact that he is in such a lower stance, the elegance and craftiness of the movement does not work its trick, making the character less capable than the amateur swordsman. After making a huge leap and regrouping the strength, the character chops off the right arm of the amateur.

✦中　　譯✦ 由於他是處在較低的姿勢，動作的優雅和精妙處無法發揮出效果，讓角色的能力看起來比起業餘的劍士更為不如。在使出大跳躍和重組攻勢後，這個角色斬斷了業餘劍士的右臂。

✦解　　析✦ 這個句型中介紹了 due to the fact that，重點在於 due to the fact that 和 due to 之間的區隔，due to 後要加名詞或名詞片語，但是 due to the fact that 後面要加子句。錯誤的地方在 Due to he is in such a lower stance, the elegance and craftiness of the movement does not work its trick，due to 要改成 due to the fact that 才合乎語法。另一個錯誤在 making the character capable than，要修正成 less capable 才符合語法。

✦檢測考點✦ 慣用語 due to the fact that 和 due to 的差異性。

佳句複誦

Due to the fact that he is in such a lower stance, the elegance and craftiness of the movement does not work its trick, making the character **less capable** than the amateur swordsman. After making a huge leap and regrouping the strength, the character chops off the right arm of the amateur.

Unit 118
慣用語 ❾：in fact「事實上 ...」

正誤句

KEY118

✖ In fact, numerous sects are eyeing for the lost martial arts skills, so rescuing those in need is just a way to cover their agendas. Evil characters using good deeds to cover the bad things they do is pretty common in the fiction, so you might have to rethink the saying "to see is to believe".

○ In fact, numerous sects are eyeing for the lost martial arts skills, so rescuing those in need is just a way to cover their agendas. Evil characters using good deeds to cover the bad things they do are pretty common in the fiction, so you might have to rethink the saying "to see is to believe".

✦中　　譯✦ 實際上，為數眾多的派別正著眼於遺失的武功，所以救援那些需要幫助的人只是掩蓋他們心機的手段。在小說中，邪惡的角色使用良善的行為去掩蓋他們做的壞事是相當司空見慣的，所以你可能必須要重新思考「眼見為憑」這個俗諺。

✦解　　析✦ 這個句型中介紹了 in fact，句子中的主要主詞為 sects，其後的動詞為複數動詞 are，so 後面的句子使用的動名詞當主詞，其後加上單數動詞 is，這部分也沒問題。Evil characters using good deeds to cover the bad things they do is pretty common in the fiction，錯誤的地方在次句，is 要改成 **are** 才合乎語法。

✦檢測考點✦ 慣用語、單複數、對等連接詞、指示代名詞後單複數。

佳句複誦

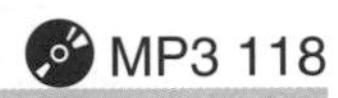

In fact, numerous sects are eyeing for the lost martial arts skills, so rescuing those in need is just a way to cover their agendas. Evil characters using good deeds to cover the bad things they do is pretty common in the fiction, so you might have to rethink the saying “to see is to believe”.

Unit 119
慣用語 ⑩：amount to 總計 +less than 的表達

正誤句

KEY 119

✗ Despite yearly earnings from Best Zoo amounted to less than 40% of those of Best Film, Best Corporation still poured lots of effort and capital into it because operation of an establishment that includes numerous wild animals was how it started the business.

○ Despite the fact that yearly earnings from Best Zoo amounted to less than 40% of those of Best Film, Best Corporation still poured lots of effort and capital into it because operation of an establishment that includes numerous wild animals was how it started the business.

✦中　　譯✦ 儘管倍斯特動物園的年利潤比倍斯特電影少百分之四十，倍斯特公司仍投注許多努力和資金在倍斯特動物園，因為營運包含為數眾多野生動物的機構是它如何草創事業的開端。

✦解　　析✦ 這個句型中介紹了 amount to，錯誤的地方在於 **Despite** yearly earnings from Best Zoo amounted to less than 40%，despite 要改成 despite the fact that，因為句子後加的是**子句**。另外要注意的是，amounted to 後面要加的是 less than 表示少了的比較使用，those 則是代替前面的 earnings。還有一個需要注意的地方是 poured lots of effort and capital into it，it 指的是 Best Zoo。

✦檢測考點✦ 慣用語（amount to）、比較級、代名詞指代。

佳句複誦

Despite the fact that yearly earnings from Best Zoo **amounted to** less than 40% of those of Best Film, Best Corporation still poured lots of effort and capital into it because operation of an establishment that includes numerous wild animals was how it started the business.

Unit 120
高階名詞當主詞 ❶：reliance on「仰賴 ...」

正誤句

KEY 120

Reliance on metabolism is still not enough to dilute the amount of toxin in the blood vessel, so consuming some herbs is quite essential. Often those herbs are located in places unattainable and are extremely rare, so peculiarity makes it expensive.

Reliance on metabolism is still not enough to dilute the amount of toxin in the blood vessel, so consuming some herbs is quite essential. Often those herbs are located in places unattainable and are extremely rare, so peculiarity makes them expensive.

✦中　　譯✦ 仰賴代謝仍不足以稀釋掉在血管中的毒素量，攝食一些草藥是相當重要的。通常那些草藥位於難抵達的地方且非常罕有，所以奇特性導致它們價格昂貴。

✦解　　析✦ 這個句型中介紹了 reliance on，用高階名詞比使用片語（rely on）形容好，建議可以多使用這樣的句型。句中的主詞是 reliance，故句子中的動詞要用單數動詞 is。So 之後的句子使用了動名詞當主詞，動詞要使用單數 is。錯誤的地方在 peculiarity makes it expensive，it 要修正為 them，因為是指代 herbs。

✦檢測考點✦ 慣用語（reliance on）、so 的用法。

佳句複誦

MP3 120

Reliance on metabolism is still not enough to dilute the amount of toxin in the blood vessel, so consuming some herbs is quite essential. Often those herbs are located in places unattainable and are extremely rare, so peculiarity makes **them** expensive.

Unit 121 高階名詞當主詞❷：familiarity with「熟悉 ...」

正誤句

KEY 121

In the fiction, familiarity with a great deal of poison can give a character several advantages, whereas proficiency in it makes someone invincible. Concealed weapons with poison can kill the enemy in a few seconds without fight.

In the fiction, familiarity with a great deal of poison can give a character several advantages, whereas proficiency in it makes someone invincible. Concealed weapons with poison can kill the enemy in a few seconds without fighting.

✦中　　譯✦ 在小說中，熟悉大量的毒藥能給一個角色幾項優點，而精通其一能使得一個人無堅不摧。餵有毒的暗器能在幾秒內不戰即殺死敵人。

✦解　　析✦ 這個句型中介紹了 familiarity with，句中的主要主詞為 familiarity，使用 a great deal of 修飾不可數名詞 poison，whereas 後主詞為 proficiency，it 指代前句的 posion，動詞使用單數的 makes。錯誤的地方在 kill the enemy in a few seconds without fight，fight 要改成 fighting 才合乎語法。

✦檢測考點✦ 慣用語（familiarity with）、whereas 的用法。

佳句複誦

MP3 121

In the fiction, familiarity with a great deal of poison can give a character several advantages, **whereas** proficiency in **it** makes someone invincible. Concealed weapons with poison can kill the enemy in a few seconds without fighting.

Unit 122
高階名詞當主詞❸：inability「無法…」

正誤句

KEY 122

✖ Assassins do pose a threat to several famous sects. His inability to withstand a series of attack by multiple swordsmen has made several masters questioned his capability to guard expensive jewelry on the way back to the Silk Road.

◯ Assassins do pose a threat to several famous sects. His inability to withstand a series of attack by multiple swordsmen has made several masters question his capability to guard expensive jewelry on the way back to the Silk Road.

✦中　　譯✦ 刺客確實對於幾個有名的門派造成威脅。他無法抵擋由武士所發動的一系列攻擊已使得幾位大師質疑，在回絲路途中他是否能保衛昂貴珠寶的能力。

✦解　　析✦ 這個句型中介紹了 inability，首句的主要主詞為 assassins，句中的動詞為 do pose，次句的句中動詞為 has made，其後要使用原形動詞，但是在錯誤句 multiple swordsmen has made several masters **questioned** his capability 中卻使用了 questioned，要將其修正為 question 才合乎語法。

✦檢測考點✦ Inability 當主詞、慣用語。

佳句複誦

MP3 122

Assassins do **pose a threat to** several famous sects. His inability to withstand a series of attack by multiple swordsmen has made several masters **question** his capability to guard expensive jewelry on the way back to the Silk Road.

Unit 123
高階名詞當主詞❹：inclination「傾向…」

正誤句

KEY 123

✖ His inclination of traversing through the Gobi Desert, even though it will be more time-consuming and labor, eventually pays off. He garnered a great straight sword under a hidden cave during the time in the Gobi Desert, and received the sacred ring that can withstand venom of all creature.

○ His inclination of traversing through the Gobi Desert, even though it will be more time-consuming and laborious, eventually pays off. He garnered a great straight sword under a hidden cave during the time in the Gobi Desert, and received the sacred ring that can withstand venom of all creatures.

中　　譯 即使這是較耗時間且費力之舉，他傾向越過戈壁沙漠最終有了回報。在戈壁沙漠期間，他在隱藏洞穴底下獲得了一把極佳的長劍，而且收到能抵禦所有物種毒素的神聖戒指。

解　　析 這個句型中介紹了 inclination，句中的動詞為 pays，只是將 even though 拉到句中而已，主要子句的敘述在後方。錯誤的地方在 even though it will be more time-consuming and labor，須將 labor 改成形容詞 **laborious** 才合乎語法。另一個錯誤的地方在 the sacred ring that can withstand venom of all **creature**，creature 要改成 creatures 才合乎語法。

檢測考點 inclination 當主詞、慣用語、even though 的用法。

佳句複誦

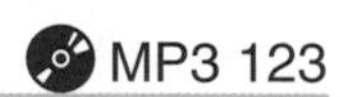

His inclination of traversing through the Gobi Desert, even though it will be more time-consuming and **laborious**, eventually pays off. He garnered a great straight sword under a hidden cave during the time in the Gobi Desert, and received the sacred ring that can withstand venom of all **creatures**.

Unit 124
高階名詞當主詞❺：likelihood「可能性…」

正誤句

KEY 124

The likelihood of meeting with numerous swordsmen is quite slim because lots of them are dissuaded by roadblocks in the labyrinth. Although this shows a little promise to the character, there are still enormous challenges that lies ahead.

The likelihood of meeting with numerous swordsmen is quite slim because lots of them are dissuaded by roadblocks in the labyrinth. Although this shows a little promise to the character, there are still enormous challenges that lie ahead.

✦中　　譯✦ 遇見為數眾多劍士的可能性是相當微乎其微的，因為他們大多數都被迷宮中的路障所阻礙住了。儘管這讓主角有了些微的希望，但是在前方仍有巨大的挑戰等著他。

✦解　　析✦ 這個句型中介紹了 likelihood，句中的主詞為 likelihood，句中動詞為 is。Because 子句內的代名詞 them 代替前面的 swordsmen。句子中錯誤的地方在 there are still enormous challenges that lies ahead，lies 要改成 lie 才合乎語法，因為 challenges 為複數名詞故要用 that lie 來修飾。

✦檢測考點✦ likelihood 當主詞、被動語態、although 的用法。

佳句複誦

The likelihood of meeting with numerous swordsmen is quite slim because lots of them are dissuaded by roadblocks in the labyrinth. Although this shows a little promise to the character, there are still enormous challenges **that lie** ahead.

Unit 125
Where 搭配複雜句型

正誤句

KEY 125

Two cheetahs are trying to find a serene place which they can enjoy the feast of the male impala without annoying thieves, such as hyenas. All of a sudden, a herd of elephants is approaching, and now they have to take a detour to the high bush.

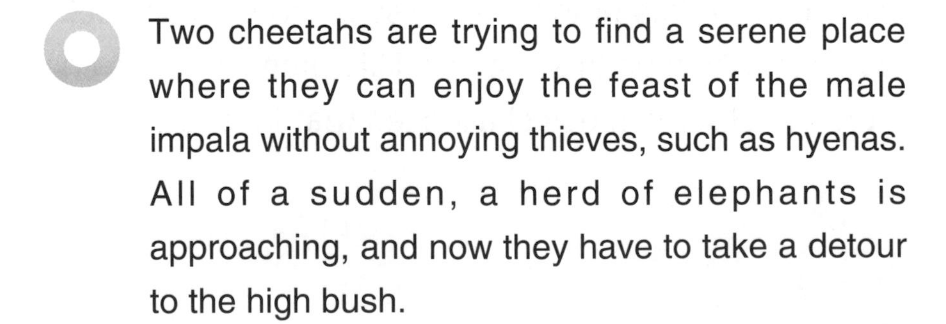

Two cheetahs are trying to find a serene place where they can enjoy the feast of the male impala without annoying thieves, such as hyenas. All of a sudden, a herd of elephants is approaching, and now they have to take a detour to the high bush.

✦中　　譯✦ 兩隻獵豹正試圖找尋牠們能享用雄性黑斑羚盛宴，且沒有擾人的小偷，例如土狼的一個寧靜的地方。突然之間，一群大象正迫近，而現在牠們必須要繞道到高灌木那裏。

✦解　　析✦ 這個句型中介紹了 where，句型中錯的地方在 Two cheetahs are trying to find a serene place **which** they can enjoy the feast of the male impala without annoying thieves, such as hyenas，which 要改成 where/in which 才合乎語法。另外要注意的地方是 without 後面要加 ving。

✦檢測考點✦ 不定詞的用法、where 的用法、without 的用法。

佳句複誦

MP3 125

Two cheetahs are trying to find a serene place where they can enjoy the feast of the male impala without annoying thieves, such as hyenas. All of a sudden, a herd of elephants is approaching, and now they have to take a detour to the high bush.

Unit 126
Before 搭配複雜句型

正誤句

KEY 126

Before fixating its eyes on a swift forest lizard, the deadly snake initiates the attack to a chameleon which just finished up the meal. Faced with an unavoidable attack, the chameleon panic, staying motionlessly on the forest floor, and the end is predictable.

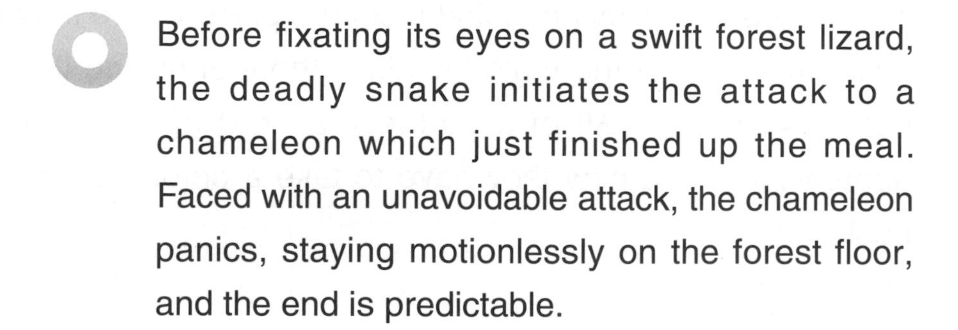

Before fixating its eyes on a swift forest lizard, the deadly snake initiates the attack to a chameleon which just finished up the meal. Faced with an unavoidable attack, the chameleon panics, staying motionlessly on the forest floor, and the end is predictable.

✦中　　譯✦ 在將目光鎖定在快速的森林蜥蜴之前，致命的毒蛇對剛結束餐點的變色龍發起了攻擊。面臨無可閃避的攻擊，變色龍感到驚慌失措，靜止地待在森林底層，而結果是可以預測到的。

✦解　　析✦ 這個句型中介紹了 before 的用法，before 後加了 ving，主要子句的主詞為 snake，主要的動詞為 initiates，其後的 chameleon 用形容詞子句修飾其剛完成餐點。次句使用分詞構句 faced with，主要子句主詞為 chameleon，錯誤句中的動詞卻誤用成複數動詞 **panic**，但是要改成單數動詞 panics 才合乎語法。

✦檢測考點✦ Before 和 after 之間的區隔處、代名詞指代、主動詞一致、過去分詞構句。

佳句複誦

MP3 126

Before fixating its eyes on a swift forest lizard, the deadly snake initiates the attack to a chameleon which just finished up the meal. Faced with an unavoidable attack, the chameleon **panics**, staying motionlessly on the forest floor, and the end is predictable.

Unit 127
After 搭配複雜句型

正誤句

KEY 127

After the long chase, the male impala exerts their one last strength, trying to overturn the fate of his own. Luckily, the horn of the male impala slightly gash the abdomen of the cheetah, forcing the cheetah to step aside.

After the long chase, the male impala exerts its one last strength, trying to overturn the fate of his own. Luckily, the horn of the male impala slightly gashes the abdomen of the cheetah, forcing the cheetah to step aside.

✦中　　譯✦ 在漫長的追逐後，雄性的黑斑羚使盡最後的力氣，試圖要翻轉牠自己的命運。幸運的是，雄性黑斑羚的角輕微地劃破了獵豹的腹部，迫使獵豹讓開。

✦解　　析✦ 這個句型中介紹了 after 的用法，錯誤句中誤用了 the male impala exerts their one last strength, trying to overturn the fate of his own.，依句意和語法，impala 指的是單數名詞，所以要將 their 改成 its 才是正確的。另外一個需要注意的地方是，次句的主詞為 horn，故動詞要使用單數動詞 gashes，且修飾動詞時要使用副詞，故要用 slightly。

✦檢測考點✦ After 的用法、慣用語。

佳句複誦

After the long chase, the male impala **exerts its one last strength**, trying to overturn the fate of his own. Luckily, the horn of the male impala **slightly gashes** the abdomen of the cheetah, forcing the cheetah to **step aside**.

Unit 128
Despite 搭配複雜句型

正誤句

KEY 128

○ Despite a series of setbacks, five female lions regroup in the place where hundreds of buffalos roam, hoping to make the kill in the next hunt. Fortunately, one of the female lions captures a calf, which is far lagged behind the herd.

✕ Despite a series of setbacks, five female lions regroup in the place where hundreds of buffalos roam, hoping to make the kill in the next hunt. Fortunately, one of the female lions capture a calf, which is far lagged behind the herd.

✦中　　譯✦ 儘管一系列的挫折，五隻雌性獅子重新部署在數百隻水牛漫步的地方，希望在下次的獵殺行動中有所斬獲。幸運的是，其中一隻雌性獅子捕獲了一頭遠落後於牛群的小牛。

✦解　　析✦ 這個句型中介紹了 despite 的用法，despite 後加 a series of setbacks，合乎語法。主要子句主詞中 lions 為複數，其動詞 regroup 為複數，在 place 後搭配 where 使用...hope to 後加原形動詞。錯誤句誤用 one of the female lions capture a calf, which is far lagged behind the herd.，capture 要改成 captures 才合乎語法。

✦檢測考點✦ Despite 的用法、where 的用法、one of…的用法。

佳句複誦

Despite a series of setbacks, five female lions regroup in the place where hundreds of buffalos roam, hoping to make the kill in the next hunt. Fortunately, one of the female lions **captures** a calf, which is far lagged behind the herd.

Unit 129
Whereas+ 形容詞子句

正誤句

KEY 129

Baby penguins which make their boldest attempt trying to swim to open sea will ultimately have a higher survival rate, whereas timid one which still linger on the coast wanting to stay safe will eventually die.

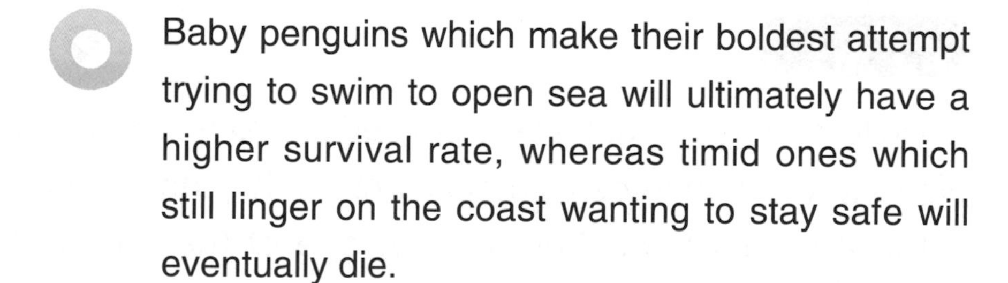

Baby penguins which make their boldest attempt trying to swim to open sea will ultimately have a higher survival rate, whereas timid ones which still linger on the coast wanting to stay safe will eventually die.

✦中　　譯✦ 試圖大膽游向開放海洋的嬰孩企鵝最終會有著較高的生存機率，而仍在海岸邊徘徊、想要維持安全貌的膽怯者最終會死亡。

✦解　　析✦ 這個句型中介紹了 whereas 較複雜句式的用法。首句主詞為 penguins 其後加關係代名詞子句 which make...而主要動詞是 will have...，whereas 引導另一個子句，錯誤句誤用在 whereas timid one which still linger on the coast wanting to stay safe will eventually die，one 要改成 ones 才合乎語法，ones 才能代替 penguins 表示複數的膽小企鵝。

✦檢測考點✦ 形容詞子句的用法、whereas 的用法、代名詞指代。

佳句複誦

Baby penguins which make their boldest attempt trying to swim to open sea will ultimately have a higher survival rate, whereas timid **ones** which still linger on the coast wanting to stay safe will eventually die.

Unit 130
As 搭配複雜句型

正誤句

KEY 130

As more and more wildebeests and zebras stride towards the Nile River, clarity of the current is becoming increasingly turbid, making Nile crocodiles thrilled. Some have captured several zebras, but its greedy nature forces them to drag more animals in the river.

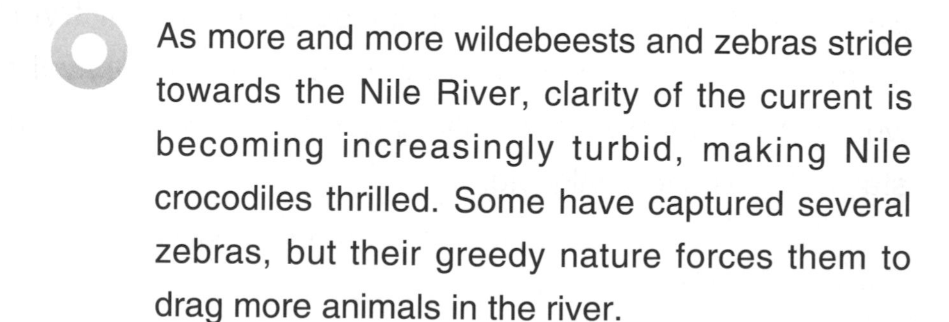

As more and more wildebeests and zebras stride towards the Nile River, clarity of the current is becoming increasingly turbid, making Nile crocodiles thrilled. Some have captured several zebras, but their greedy nature forces them to drag more animals in the river.

✦中　　譯✦ 當越來越多的牛羚和斑馬朝著尼羅河闊步，水流的清晰度正逐漸變得混濁，讓尼羅河鱷魚興奮異常。有些已經捕獲了幾隻斑馬，但是鱷魚貪婪的天性迫使牠們拖曳更多動物到河裡頭。

✦解　　析✦ 這個句型中 as...as 搭配 more and more 的用法，首句的副詞子句中主詞為 **wildebeests and zebras**，動詞為 **stride**，主要子句中以現在進行式表達，表示因牛羚和斑馬的越河使得河水漸漸變得混濁。錯誤句的發生在 but its greedy nature forces them to drag more animals in the river.，its 要改成 their 才合乎語意和語法。

✦檢測考點✦ As 的用法、make 的用法、時態、but 的用法。

佳句複誦

MP3 130

As more and more wildebeests and zebras stride towards the Nile River, clarity of the current is **becoming increasingly turbid**, making Nile crocodiles **thrilled**. Some have captured several zebras, but **their** greedy nature forces them to drag more animals in the river.

Unit 131
During 搭配複雜句型

正誤句

KEY 131

During the chase, the giraffe unexpectedly lashes out, giving a fatal kick right in the abdomen of the cheetah. The sound made by the cheetah is unbearable. The stomach of the cheetah churn, oozing blood through other parts of the body.

During the chase, the giraffe unexpectedly lashes out, giving a fatal kick right in the abdomen of the cheetah. The sound made by the cheetah is unbearable. The stomach of the cheetah churns, oozing blood through other parts of the body.

✦中　　譯✦ 在追逐期間，長頸鹿出乎意料之外的突然猛擊，給予致命的一擊正中獵豹腹部。獵豹所發出的聲音令人難以忍受。獵豹的胃部翻騰，滲出血液，流至身體其他部位。

✦解　　析✦ 這個句型中介紹了 during 用以表示一段時間，首句的主詞為 giraffe 其後加上單數動詞 lashes。次句的主詞為 sound，其後省略 which is，句中主要動詞為 is。錯誤句的發生在 The stomach of the cheetah churn, oozing blood through other parts of the body，churn 要改成 churns 才合乎語法。

✦檢測考點✦ During 的用法、慣用語。

佳句複誦

MP3 131

During the chase, the giraffe **unexpectedly lashes out**, giving a fatal kick right in the abdomen of the cheetah. The sound made by the cheetah is unbearable. The stomach of the cheetah **churns**, oozing blood through other parts of the body.

Unit 132
No matter 搭配複雜句型

正誤句

KEY 132

However robust a lion can be, an injury during the chase or the hunt can make the fate of the lion doomed. Lions does not have a doctor, and any infection in the wound can be quite deadly.

No matter how robust a lion can be, an injury during the chase or the hunt can make the fate of the lion doomed. Lions do not have a doctor, and any infection in the wound can be quite deadly.

✦中　　譯✦ 不論獅子有多麼健壯，在追逐期間或狩獵時所受的傷都能讓獅子的毀滅。獅子沒有醫生，而傷口處的任何感染都能是相當致命的。

✦解　　析✦ 在這個句型中，no matter how=however，表示「無論如何」的意思，所以兩個句子的開頭均無誤。句中的主詞為 injury，主要動詞為 can make，且 the fate of the lion 後以 doomed 當補語。錯誤句的發生在 Lions does not have a doctor, and any infection in the wound can be quite deadly.，does 要改成 do 才合乎語法，因為 lions 為複數名詞。

✦檢測考點✦ No matter 的用法。

佳句複誦

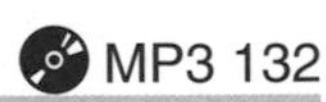

No matter how robust a lion can be, an injury during the chase or the hunt can make the fate of the lion doomed. Lions **do not** have a doctor, and any infection in the wound can be quite deadly.

Unit 133
Whenever 搭配複雜句型

KEY 133

Whenever the male lion cub finds anything novelty around him, his curiosity evokes from within and he tries to understand what is the object. This can be a good thing because the more he learns, the better he becomes.

Whenever the male lion cub finds anything novel around him, his curiosity evokes from within and he tries to understand what the object is. This can be a good thing because the more he learns, the better he becomes.

✦中　　譯✦ 每當雄性獅子幼獸發現牠周遭任何新奇的東西，心中內部喚起牠的好奇心，牠試圖了解物品是什麼東西。這對牠來說是件好事，因為牠學習的更多，牠就能成就更好的自我。

✦解　　析✦ 這個句型中介紹了 whenever 的用法，子句中的主詞為 cub，其後動詞為 finds，錯誤的地方在 finds anything novelty around him，novelty 要改成形容詞 novel 才合乎語法。另一個錯誤的地方在 he tries to understand what is the object，what is the object 要改成 what the object is 才合乎語法。

✦檢測考點✦ Whenever 的用法、慣用語、what 的用法。

佳句複誦

MP3 133

Whenever the male lion cub finds anything **novel** around him, his curiosity evokes from within and he tries to understand what the object is. This can be a good thing because the more he learns, the better he becomes.

Unit 134
So...that 搭配複雜句型

正誤句

KEY 134

The eggs of the ostrich are so bigness that it is hard to smuggle numerous of the eggs in a narrow pathway. One possible way is to traverse a different route, which involve taking a sea road.

The eggs of the ostrich are so big that it is hard to smuggle numerous of the eggs in a narrow pathway. One possible way is to traverse a different route, which involves taking a sea road.

✦中　　譯✦ 鴕鳥的蛋是如此的大顆以致於其經由狹窄的通道中要走私為數眾多的蛋是很難的。其中一個可能的辦法是從不同的路徑橫越，此牽涉到要走海路。

✦解　　析✦ 這個句型中介紹了 so...that 的用法，首句的主詞為 eggs，句中的動詞為 are，錯誤的地方在 The eggs of the ostrich are so bigness that it is，bigness 要改為形容詞 big 才合乎語法。另一個錯誤的地方在 One possible way is to traverse a different route, which involve taking a sea road.，involve 要改成 involves 才合乎語法。

✦檢測考點✦ So...that 的用法、形容詞子句。

佳句複誦

The eggs of the ostrich are so big that it is hard to smuggle numerous of the eggs in a narrow pathway. One possible way is to traverse a different route, which **involves** taking a sea road.

Unit 135
Enable 搭配複雜句型

正誤句

KEY 135

The height of the giraffe enables it to consume food on exceedingly high branches, a meal that is unattainable to most herbivores. Elephants, like giraffes, is also benefited from having tallness and their trunks allow them to grab twigs and leaves on high boughs.

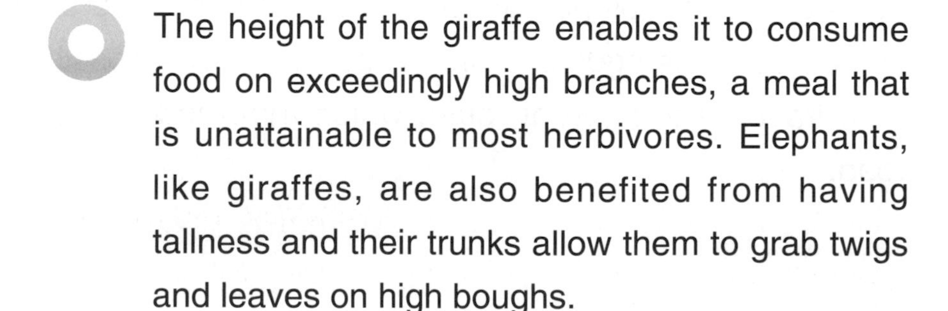

The height of the giraffe enables it to consume food on exceedingly high branches, a meal that is unattainable to most herbivores. Elephants, like giraffes, are also benefited from having tallness and their trunks allow them to grab twigs and leaves on high boughs.

✦中　譯✦ 長頸鹿的高度使其能夠攝食在極高樹枝上的食物，這個餐點對於大多數的草食性動物來說是無法實現的。大象，如同長頸鹿一樣，也受惠於有著高大的身軀，且牠們的象鼻使牠們能夠獲取高處大樹枝上的樹枝和葉子。

✦解　析✦ 這個句型中介紹了 enable 的用法，首句中的主詞為 height，句中的動詞為 enables，其後以 it 指代 giraffe，在 consume food 後也以副詞+形容詞的形式修飾 branches，其後更以同位語補充說明。錯誤的地方在 Elephants, like giraffes, is also benefited from having tallness and their trunks allow them to grab twigs and leaves on high boughs.，is 要改成 are 才合乎語法，因為 elephants 為複數名詞。

✦檢測考點✦ Enable 的用法、同位語的用法、like 的用法、同義詞轉換。

佳句複誦

MP3 135

The **height** of the giraffe enables it **to consume** food on exceedingly high branches, a meal that is **unattainable** to most herbivores. Elephants, **like** giraffes, **are** also benefited from having tallness and their trunks **allow** them **to** grab twigs and leaves on high boughs.

Unit 136
As long as 搭配複雜句型

正誤句

KEY 136

As long as the predator makes a killing bite, the prey usually suffocates in an instant and dies. Immature and inexperienced predators is often struggling to make a killing bite, so it is highly likely that the prey might run away almost unharmed.

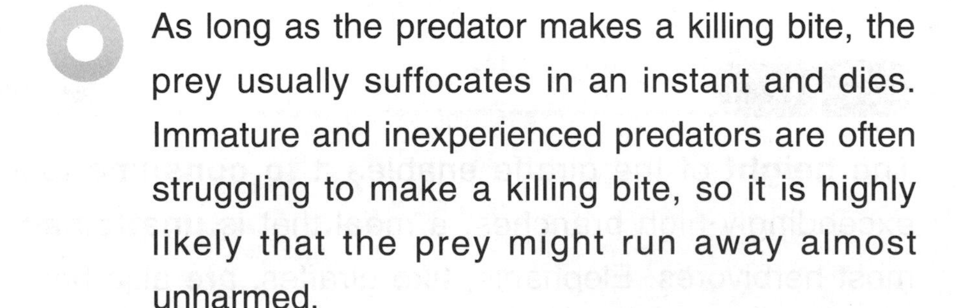

As long as the predator makes a killing bite, the prey usually suffocates in an instant and dies. Immature and inexperienced predators are often struggling to make a killing bite, so it is highly likely that the prey might run away almost unharmed.

✦中　　譯✦ 只要掠食者使出致命之咬，獵物通常一下子就窒息且死亡了。不成熟且毫無經驗的掠食者通常掙扎著而無法使出致命之咬，所以獵物有極高的可能會幾近毫髮無傷的逃跑。

✦解　　析✦ 這個句型中介紹了 as long as 的用法，副詞子句中的主詞為 the predator，動詞為 makes，主要子句中的主詞為 prey，主要動詞為 suffocates 和 dies。錯誤的地方在次句 Immature and inexperienced predators is often struggling to make a killing bite，is 要改成 **are** 才合乎語法，因為 predators 為複數名詞。

✦檢測考點✦ As long as 的用法、so 的用法。

佳句複誦

As long as the predator makes a killing bite, the prey usually suffocates in an instant and dies. Immature and inexperienced predators **are** often struggling to make a killing bite, so it is highly likely that the prey might run away almost unharmed.

Unit 137
Unless 搭配複雜句型

正誤句

KEY 137

The chameleon is lacking the luster when it comes to fighting with the zebra snake. The zebra snake is nimbler than the chameleon, so it outruns the chameleon. Unless the chameleon is able to outwit the zebra snake, their fate is anticipated to numerous visitors in Best Zoo.

The chameleon is lacking the luster when it comes to fighting with the zebra snake. The zebra snake is nimbler than the chameleon, so it outruns the chameleon. Unless the chameleon is able to outwit the zebra snake, its fate is anticipated to numerous visitors in Best Zoo.

✦中　　譯✦ 當提到與斑馬蛇的對戰，變色龍顯得光芒黯淡。斑馬蛇比變色龍更為敏捷，所以牠跑得比變色龍更快。對於在倍斯特動物園中為數眾多的觀光客來說，除非變色龍能夠智勝斑馬蛇，牠的命運是可預期的。

✦解　　析✦ 這個句型中介紹了 unless 的用法，首句中的主詞為 chameleon，主要動詞為 is，其後搭配 when it comes to，其後要加 Ving or 名詞。次句的主詞為 snake，動詞是 is，so 之後以 it 代替 snake。錯誤的地方在 Unless the chameleon is able to outwit the zebra snake, their fate is anticipated to numerous visitors in Best Zoo.，their 要改成 its 才合乎語法。

✦檢測考點✦ when it comes to 的用法、比較級、unless 的用法。

佳句複誦

MP3 137

The chameleon is lacking the luster when it comes to fighting with the zebra snake. The zebra snake is nimbler than the chameleon, so it outruns the chameleon. Unless the chameleon is able to outwit the zebra snake, **its** fate is anticipated to numerous visitors in Best Zoo.

Unit 138
過去分詞構句

正誤句

KEY 138

✗ Equipped with potent venom as a powerful weapon and native to the North and South America, rattlesnakes are marked by its tails for producing buzzing sounds. These sounds are the warnings, but not all creatures are afraid of the formidable predators.

○ Equipped with potent venom as a powerful weapon and native to the North and South America, rattlesnakes are marked by their tails for producing buzzing sounds. These sounds are the warnings, but not all creatures are afraid of the formidable predators.

✦中　　譯✦ 裝配強而有力的毒素當作其強大的武器且原產於北美洲和南美洲，響尾蛇以牠們尾部會產生嗡嗡的聲響為其特徵。這些聲音是種警告，但是並非所有的生物都懼怕這個令人敬畏的掠食者。

✦解　　析✦ 這個句型中介紹了 be equipped with 和 native to 的用法，在單元例句中以過去分詞構句的形式呈現出並搭配 native to。首句中，主要子句的主詞為 rattlesnakes，動詞為 are。錯誤的地方在 rattlesnakes are marked by its tails for producing buzzing sounds，its 要改成 their 才合乎語法，因為主詞 rattlesnakes 為複數名詞。

✦檢測考點✦ 慣用語（be equipped with 和 native to）、but 的用法。

佳句複誦

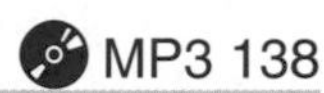

Equipped with potent venom as a powerful weapon and native to the North and South America, rattlesnakes **are marked by their** tails for producing buzzing sounds. These sounds are the warnings, but not all creatures are afraid of the formidable predators.

Unit 139
現在分詞構句

正誤句

KEY 139

Initially serving as the breeding ground for most tree frogs due to its muddy and marshy habitat, and abundant migratory locusts, the forest is now overwhelmed these green amphibians.

Initially serving as the breeding ground for most tree frogs due to its muddy and marshy habitat, and abundant migratory locusts, the forest is now overwhelmed by these green amphibians.

✦中　　譯✦ 由於泥濘和沼澤般的棲地，起初能充當起大多數樹蛙的繁殖場所和豐盛的遷徙而來的蝗蟲，森林現在被這些綠色的兩棲生物所掩沒了。

✦解　　析✦ 這個句型中介紹了「現在分詞構句」的用法，其實可以搭配的片語有非常多，考生在寫作中可以使用這個句型增添句式豐富度。在原有的【Ving.., S+V...】架構中間又插入了 due to…更充分說明了「原因」，due to 後的 its 指代主要子句的主詞 the forest，表示其泥濘和沼澤般的棲地。錯誤的地方是 the forest is now overwhelmed these green amphibians.，is overwhelmed 要將其改成 is overwhelmed by 才合乎被動語態的語法。如果要使用主動的話，則要將其改成 overwhelms。

✦檢測考點✦ 現在分詞構句的用法、due to 的用法。

佳句複誦

MP3 139

Initially serving as the breeding ground for most tree frogs due to its muddy and marshy habitat, and abundant migratory locusts, the forest is now overwhelmed by these green amphibians.

Unit 140
倒裝句 ❶：主詞和副詞片語調換位置

正誤句

KEY 140

Through an exceedingly large five-colored clam's twenty years of nurturing have developed a rare pearl, uniquely-crafted and dazzling, and it can be hardly attained through a normal search and is guarded by predators, such as venomous bacteria.

Through an exceedingly large five-colored clam's twenty years of nurturing has developed a rare pearl, uniquely-crafted and dazzling, and it can be hardly attained through a normal search and is guarded by predators, such as venomous bacteria.

✦中　譯✦ 獨特巧妙地製作成且暈眩奪目的罕見珍珠，是透過極大型五彩蚌經由 20 年的孕育而發展成的，而且很難透過慣有的方式取得，加上受到像是有毒細菌這樣的掠食者所保衛著。

✦解　析✦ 這題需要掌握倒裝句和主動詞的區分，主要的主詞是 pearl，故動詞要使用 has，但句型經由倒裝後容易造成誤判，進而選到或使用了錯誤的時態。原句是 A rare pearl, uniquely-crafted and dazzling has developed through an exceedingly large five-colored clam's twenty years of nurturing, and it can be hardly attained through a normal search and is guarded by predators, such as venomous bacteria.。

✦檢測考點✦ 倒裝句的用法、through 的用法、表列舉。

佳句複誦

Through an exceedingly large five-colored clam's twenty years of nurturing has developed a rare pearl, uniquely-crafted and dazzling, and it can be hardly attained through a normal search and is guarded by predators, such as venomous bacteria

Unit 141
rich in, result from 和數個形容詞子句

正誤句

KEY 141

An avenue rich in diverse food resources, such as a sudden swarm of locusts and numerous insects that attract multitudinous tree frogs to gather here has resulted from drastic climate changes that brings so many insects.

An avenue rich in diverse food resources, such as a sudden swarm of locusts and numerous insects that attract multitudinous tree frogs to gather here has resulted from drastic climate changes that bring so many insects.

✦中　　譯✦ 富含多樣食物來源，例如突然蜂擁而至的蝗蟲和為數眾多的昆蟲，吸引著大量的樹蛙聚集此地，導因於急遽的氣候變化，以致引來許多昆蟲。

✦解　　析✦ 這個句型中介紹了 rich in 和 result from 兩個常見的片語。首句主詞為 avenue，其後使用了關係代名詞子句，當中省略了 which is，再加上表舉例的項目，其中又使用 that 子句修飾 insects 等列舉項目，句中的主要動詞為 has resulted，錯誤的地方是 to gather here has resulted from drastic climate changes that brings so many insects.，brings 要改成 bring 才合乎語法。

✦檢測考點✦ 表列舉、數個形容詞子句省略。

佳句複誦

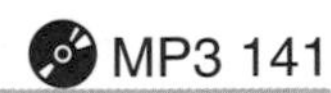

An avenue rich in diverse food resources, such as a sudden swarm of locusts and numerous insects that attract multitudinous tree frogs to gather here has resulted from drastic climate changes that bring so many insects.

Unit 142
As...as+if...(not more)

正誤句

KEY 142

The role and ability of lions can sometimes be underestimated due to their lack of speed in running, but lions are as bloodthirsty as cheetahs, if not more ferocious. In addition, they work as a team, so that makes them resilient and adaptive than other carnivores.

The role and ability of lions can sometimes be underestimated due to their lack of speed in running, but lions are as bloodthirsty as cheetahs, if not more ferocious. In addition, they work as a team, so that makes them more resilient and adaptive than other carnivores.

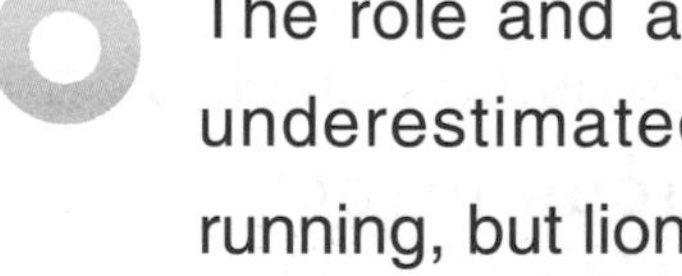

✦中　　譯✦ 獅子的角色和能力有時候可能被低估了，由於牠們在跑步時缺乏速度，但是獅子至少也與獵豹是一樣兇猛的獵者，即使牠沒有那麼兇猛。此外，獅子是團隊合作，所以這使得牠們比起其他肉食動物更有彈性且更具適應性。

✦解　　析✦ 這個句型中介紹了數個句型用法，主要的考點是 if...(not more)...的用法。首句的主詞為 role 和 ability，句中動詞為 can be underestimated，後句中的 their 指代 lions，but 後的主詞為 lions，主要的動詞為 are，且使用了 as...as 的句型。If not more 後面要使用**形容詞**。錯誤的地方是 In addition, they work as a team, so that makes them **resilient and adaptive** than other carnivores.，在 **resilient and adaptive** 前要加 more 才合乎比較級的語法。

✦檢測考點✦ due to 的用法、but 的用法、if 的用法、so that 的用法。

佳句複誦

The role and ability of lions can sometimes be underestimated due to their lack of speed in running, but lions are as bloodthirsty as cheetahs, if not more ferocious. In addition, they work as a team, so that makes them more resilient and adaptive than other carnivores.

Unit 143 As many as 多達 ... 倍數與比較級的用法

正誤句

KEY 143

In Australia, five time as many as koalas was killed in car accidents last year, and the astounding number is greater than predicted. The number of the deceased koalas was greater than dead kangaroos, perhaps due to the fact that koalas can neither run nor jump.

In Australia, five times as many as koalas were killed in car accidents last year, and the astounding number is greater than predicted. The number of the deceased koalas was greater than that of dead kangaroos, perhaps due to the fact that koalas can neither run nor jump.

✦中　　譯✦ 在澳洲，去年有多達五倍的無尾熊於車禍中喪生，而這個令人感到震驚的數字比起預測的數量更多。死亡的無尾熊數量比起死亡袋鼠的數量更多，可能由於無尾熊既不能跑也無法跳躍。

✦解　　析✦ 這個句型有倍數的表達搭配 as many as 的句型。錯誤的地方有 In Australia, five time as many as koalas was killed in car accidents last year, and the astounding number is greater than predicted.，five 之後要加上複數，所以 time 要改成 **times**，was 的部分也要更正為 **were**，因為主詞變成 times。另一個要修正的地方是 The number of the deceased koalas was greater than dead kangaroos, perhaps due to the fact that koalas can neither run nor jump.，greater than 後方需要加上 that of 才不會造成修飾上的錯誤。

✦檢測考點✦ 比較級、as many as、代名詞指代。

佳句複誦

MP3 143

In Australia, five times as many as koalas were killed in car accidents last year, and the astounding number is greater than predicted. The number of the deceased koalas was greater than that of dead kangaroos, perhaps due to the fact that koalas can neither run nor jump.

Unit 144
特殊用法：criteria+ 複數動詞、主動詞一致性

正誤句

KEY 144

✗ Criteria for selecting a mate is quite different in animals. Female impalas choose their mate by testing potential mates about their agility and speed, whereas some male birds offer gifts to please female birds.

○ Criteria for selecting a mate are quite different in animals. Female impalas choose their mate by testing potential mates about their agility and speed, whereas some male birds offer gifts to please female birds.

✦中　　譯✦ 選擇伴侶的標準對於動物來說是相當不同的。雌性黑斑羚藉由測試潛在伴侶的敏捷度和速度來選擇其伴侶，而有些雄性鳥類提供禮物去取悅雌性鳥類。

✦解　　析✦ 這個句型主要是檢視對名詞的掌握，有些特殊的名詞並非以複數形式結尾，但是需視為是「複數的主詞」，故要使用複數動詞才合乎語法。在句子中，看到 criteria 後，馬上跳到動詞 are 來檢視**「主動詞一致性」**，句子是合乎語法的，而錯誤句中，卻誤用了 is 這個動詞。

✦檢測考點✦ 其他形式的複數主詞、代名詞指代。

佳句複誦

Criteria for selecting a mate are quite different in animals. Female impalas choose their mate by testing potential mates about their agility and speed, whereas some male birds offer gifts to please female birds.

Unit 145
關係代名詞 ❶：who

正誤句

KEY 145

✖ Tourists which visited Africa's Serengeti a year ago, were able to witness the epic fight between four male lions and a clan of hyenas in such a close distance. One of the male lions unexpectedly attacks the hyena from its back, and the other three male lions rush towards it and ferociously bite on three parts of the hyena body.

○ Tourists who visited Africa's Serengeti a year ago, were able to witness the epic fight between four male lions and a clan of hyenas in such a close distance. One of the male lions unexpectedly attacks the hyena from its back, and the other three male lions rush towards it and ferociously bite on three parts of the hyena body.

✦中　　譯✦ 拜訪非洲賽倫蓋蒂的觀光客能夠在如此近的距離下，目睹四隻雄性獅子和一群土狼之間壯觀的戰鬥。其中一隻雄性獅子出其不意地從土狼背後發動攻擊，而其他三隻雄性獅子衝向牠，且兇猛地往土狼的三個部位咬去。

✦解　　析✦ 這個句型主要是檢視對關係代名詞的掌握，可以由先行詞和關係代名詞作為判斷依據，這個句型中關係代名詞前的先行詞是 tourists，故要使用 who，且是 who 當主格，故不能省略，正確句合乎語法。錯誤句中關係代名詞誤用了 which，無法修飾 tourists，所以要改為 who 才合乎語法。

✦檢測考點✦ Who 的用法、時態、one of…的用法、代名詞指代。

佳句複誦

MP3 145

Tourists who visited Africa's Serengeti a year ago, were able to witness the epic fight between four male lions and a clan of hyenas in such a close distance. One of the male lions unexpectedly attacks the hyena from its back, and the other three male lions rush towards it and ferociously bite on three parts of the hyena body.

Unit 146
關係代名詞 ❷：which

正誤句

KEY 146

The chimpanzee had eaten the small monkey's brain hours earlier, tried to demonstrate his masculinity and charm. The cruelty might scare us, but the brain of the small monkey does contain nutritious contents that can benefit the growth of the chimpanzee.

The chimpanzee which had eaten the small monkey's brain hours earlier, tried to demonstrate his masculinity and charm. The cruelty might scare us, but the brain of the small monkey does contain nutritious contents that can benefit the growth of the chimpanzee.

✦中　　譯✦ 於幾小時之前吃掉小猴子大腦的黑猩猩試圖展現他雄性氣概和魅力。殘忍度可能嚇到了我們，但是小猴子腦部確實含有營養的內容物，有益於黑猩猩的成長。

✦解　　析✦ 這個句型主要是檢視對關係代名詞的掌握，可以由先行詞和關係代名詞作為判斷依據，這個句型中關係代名詞前的先行詞是黑猩猩，故使用 which，又因為是 **which 當主格，故不能省略**。錯誤句中省略了關係代名詞而造成句子中有雙動詞，不合於文法。

✦檢測考點✦ Which 的用法、but 的用法。

佳句複誦

The chimpanzee which had eaten the small monkey's brain hours earlier, tried to demonstrate his masculinity and charm. The cruelty might scare us, but the brain of the small monkey does contain nutritious contents that can benefit the growth of the chimpanzee.

Unit 147
關係代名詞 ❸：whose

正誤句

KEY 147

Two brown bears which mother unanticipatedly died by gunshot, are now forced to stand on their own feet much earlier without any parental guidance. Their first task is to find the food without getting injured or encounter any predators.

Two brown bears whose mother unanticipatedly died by gunshot, are now forced to stand on their own feet much earlier without any parental guidance. Their first task is to find the food without getting injured or encounter any predators.

✦中　　譯✦ 兩隻棕熊的母親出乎意料之外的死於槍擊之下，現在正被迫要在沒有任何父母的指導情況下獨立生活。牠們的首要任務就是要在不受到傷害或遇到任何掠食者的情況下找到食物。

✦解　　析✦ 這個句型主要是檢視對關係代名詞的掌握，可以由先行詞和關係代名詞後的**名詞**作為判斷依據，由於先行詞是棕熊，而關係代名詞後的名詞是母親/熊，所以要使用所有格 **whose**，而形成了 Two brown bears whose mother unanticipatedly died...。

✦檢測考點✦ Whose 的用法、without 的用法、副詞搭配。

佳句複誦

Two brown bears whose mother **unanticipatedly** died by gunshot, are now forced to stand on their own feet much earlier without **any parental guidance**. Their first task is to find the food without getting injured or encounter any predators.

Unit 148
關係代名詞❹：that

正誤句

KEY 148

The female lion who lingers for a few moments tries exceedingly hard to overcome the death of her newborn son. A negligence for an inexperienced lion mother can result in a situation like this.

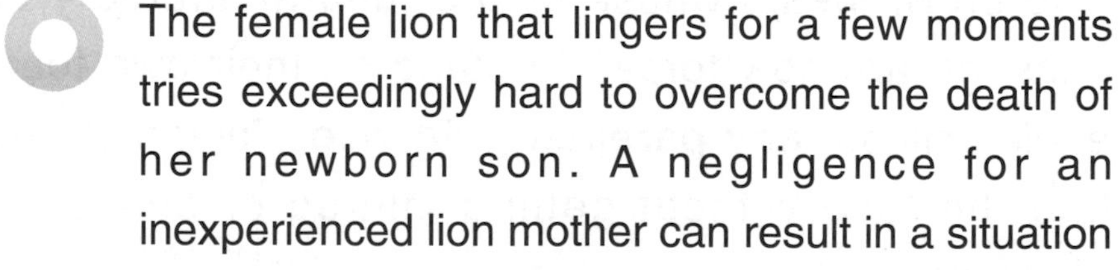

The female lion that lingers for a few moments tries exceedingly hard to overcome the death of her newborn son. A negligence for an inexperienced lion mother can result in a situation like this.

✦中　　譯✦ 雌性獅子在那裡徘徊了幾下，極力試圖克服她剛出生雄性幼獸的死亡。經驗不足的獅子母親的疏忽會導致像這樣的情況。

✦解　　析✦ 根據語法要使用 **which or that**，that 引導的子句進一步解釋主詞 the female lion，另外需要注意的部分是，要注意主詞的單複數，因為這會影響到接續關係代名詞要使用的單複數，在這個句子中為單數的主詞 lion 所以 that 之後加上單數動詞 lingers。

✦檢測考點✦ That 的用法、result in 的用法。

佳句複誦

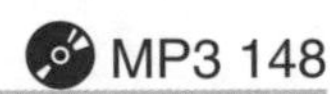

The female lion that lingers for a few moments tries exceedingly hard to overcome the death of her newborn son. A **negligence** for an inexperienced lion mother can result in a situation like this.

Unit 149
脫節修飾語 ❶

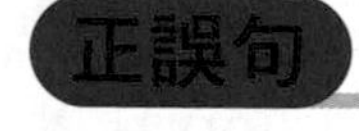

正誤句

KEY 149

After taking to the Best Animal Shelter, the injured bear experienced a 10-hour long surgery, and eventually had a heartbeat, which made veterinarians thrilled.The dose of the anesthetic now clearly subsides and the recovered bear moves its arms again.

After taken to the Best Animal Shelter, the injured bear experienced a 10-hour long surgery, and eventually had a heartbeat, which made veterinarians thrilled.The dose of the anesthetic now clearly subsides and the recovered bear moves its arms again.

✦中　譯✦ 在被帶至倍斯特動物庇護所後，受傷的熊經歷了為期 10 小時的外科手術，最終有了心跳，讓獸醫們都感到興奮。現在，麻醉劑的劑量顯然消退了，而復原的熊又開始揮動牠的手臂了。

✦解　析✦ 很容易會使用成 after taking，因為常見 after or before+V-ing 的形式，但是看到主要子句的主詞 the injured bear，可以得知其是**「被帶回」**Best Animal Shelter，是被動語態，在副詞子句中省略了(it was)，故要使用 taken。

✦檢測考點✦ 修飾語脫節、形容詞子句的用法、代名詞指代。

佳句複誦

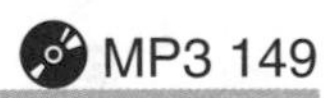

After taken to the Best Animal Shelter, the injured bear experienced a 10-hour long surgery, and eventually had a heartbeat, which made veterinarians **thrilled**. The dose of the anesthetic now clearly subsides and the **recovered** bear moves its arms again.

Unit 150
脫節修飾語 ❷

正誤句

KEY 150

Judged from the current circumstance, the head of the female lions surmised that the target, a pregnant female giraffe, would pose no more threat to them, so she initiated an attack behind the back of the giraffe, which insulated it from other giraffes.

Judging from the current circumstance, the head of the female lions surmised that the target, a pregnant female giraffe, would pose no more threat to them, so she initiated an attack behind the back of the giraffe, which insulated it from other giraffes.

✦中　　譯✦ 由現在的情況來看，雌性獅子們的首領推測目標物，即懷孕的雌性長頸鹿，對於牠們不會造成威脅，所以她從長頸鹿背後發動的攻擊，將其與其他長頸鹿隔離開來。

✦解　　析✦ 主詞 S 須能從事前面 V-ing 的動作，否則就會造成**「修飾語脫節」**的問題。將 the head of the female lions 這個主詞代回去並評定語意是否正確。而且錯誤句子使用了被動的 judged，但是根據語法要使用主動語態 judging。

✦檢測考點✦ 修飾語脫節、同位語、so 的用法。

佳句複誦

Judging from the current circumstance, the head of the female lions surmised that the target, a pregnant female giraffe, would pose no more threat to them, so she initiated an attack behind the back of the giraffe, which insulated it from other giraffes.

國家圖書館出版品預行編目(CIP)資料

一次就考到雅思文法7⁺/ 韋爾著-- 初版. --
新北市：倍斯特, 2019.12 面； 公分. --
（考用英語系列；22）
ISBN 978-986-98079-2-0（平裝附光碟）
1.國際英語語文測試系統 2.語法

805.189 108019378

考用英語系列 022

一次就考到雅思文法7⁺（附英式發音MP3）

初　　版　2019年12月
定　　價　新台幣460元

作　　者　韋爾
出　　版　倍斯特出版事業有限公司
發 行 人　周瑞德
電　　話　886-2-8245-6905
傳　　真　886-2-2245-6398
地　　址　23558 新北市中和區立業路83巷7號4樓
E-mail　best.books.service@gmail.com
官　　網　www.bestbookstw.com
總 編 輯　齊心瑀
封面構成　高鍾琪
內頁構成　菩薩蠻數位文化有限公司
印　　製　大亞彩色印刷製版股份有限公司

港澳地區總經銷　泛華發行代理有限公司
地　　址　香港新界將軍澳工業邨駿昌街7號2樓
電　　話　852-2798-2323
傳　　真　852-3181-3973